Hustle Made II:

The Book of Enoch

By: T. Marie

T. Marie
Hustle Made II: The Book of Enoch

Chapter 1

*I*nside the back of that van I knew it was over. Enoch had caught up to me right along with my past. I couldn't clear my head because of the drugs in my system and the adrenalin wearing off. I gave myself to the situation feeling that it was over for me. The van tore out of the parking lot at a high rate of speed. I felt the van make a hard turn onto the street. I was thrown up against the side of the van like a ragdoll. We couldn't have made it more than a block before the van jolted to a stop due to it crashing.

I heard multiple gunshots coming from outside the van and was sure I would be hit. I didn't care tho. I had just saw the love of my life stretched out on the floor, laying in a pool of blood, dead. I desired to be with him so I welcomed the bullet that would take my life as well. The gunshots stopped and I heard voices. I couldn't make them out nor what they were saying. I could tell it was both a male and a female and they were getting closer.

The side door of the van opened and I was snatched out and thrown to the ground. The male voice said to me. "Yeah, thought I would never catch up to you two huh bitch?" In my drug induced haze I couldn't make out the voice. But apparently he was talking to me. He then jumped into the back of the van and I heard more shots ring out. I heard the female who sounded very familiar say. "You want me to off this bitch too?"

"Nah, I got something else in store for her." The male culprit replied.

He hopped back out the van and instructed his female accomplice to help him get me to the other car. I was lifted up by my feet and my shoulders and carried like a sack of potatoes. They got me to their car and threw me in the trunk. I noticed that they had on masks and they were wearing all black. The car was smoking from under the hood due to the fact that they had used it to crash into the van. My mind was workings overtime trying to figure out what part of my past had finally caught up with me.

The drugs wouldn't allow me a clear thought, so I just gave in to the high as well as the situation I was now in. When I was in the back of the van I welcomed death, but now in the trunk of this car, all that had changed. By the way I was rolling back and forth in this trunk I could tell we were going fast as well as hitting corners. I hit my head hard on something in the trunk and lost consciousness. I was jarred awake by being roughly snatched from the trunk and thrown over the shoulder of my male captor.

I heard the familiar female voice say, "I don't know why we didn't just kill this bitch and leave her there with a bullet in her head like the other three!"

"Bitch quit your yapping and take that car and get rid of it!"

"Who you callin a bitch nigga?" was her reply.

"Babe not now!" was all he said as he changed his tone. "I am going to take this snake ass bitch in here and secure her. Then I'll be there to get you at the scrap yard. It shouldn't be more than five, ten minutes." With that being said I felt him carry me down some stairs and into what smelled like a basement.

It was cold, dank, and moldy smelling. He threw me on the ground which was just as cold as the air felt. I hit the back of my head on what had to be concrete. My ass absorbed most of the impact. I heard him pull on what sounded like one of those chains that were attached to lights that hung from the ceiling or ceiling fan. As soon as the light came on I wished it hadn't. My assumptions were correct. I was in what appeared to be some sort of basement. There was trash on the ground, what looked to be piles of clothes, some stacked up boxes; along with a box spring and mattress with no sheets on it.

There was a set of stairs that lead up into the dwelling I was in. The mystery man never said a word as he moved some of the boxes and retrieved a chain.

He then attached it to a pipe in the ceiling over the mattress area. After doing this he went up the stairs and came back with a box cutter and a set of handcuffs in his hands. He approached me as I stared at him noticing something familiar about his walk and build. I noticed the bulge in his waistband letting me know he was still strapped. He walked up to me and said nothing more than, "Don't try me!" as he reached behind me and cut the zip ties with the box cutter.

I told me to put my hands out in front of me and I complied. I asked him what it was that he wanted with me and he just peered at me with the coldest eyes I had ever seen. I don't know why but even the eyes seemed slightly familiar. "If it's money you want I can pay you, just please don't hurt or kill me!" He never even acknowledged my plea and just put the cuffs on my wrists. He picked me up again and carried me to the dirty mattress and threw me down again. I had one thought: I wished he would have threw me on here first instead of on that hard ass ground.

He took the chain now attached to the pipe in the ceiling and attached it to the cuffs on my wrists. Just when I thought the worst of what could be done was over, he pulled a package containing a syringe and a vial of something out of his pocket. He tore the package open containing the syringe, stuck it in the vial and pulled back on the syringe filling it with the clear liquid from the vial.

I instantly knew what his plans were and started begging and pleading with what little energy I had left. He didn't even seem as if he heard me as he tied what appeared to be an extension cord around my arm. He then found the vein he was looking for and shot the whole dosage of whatever was in the syringe in my arm, then untied the extension cord. The shit didn't take long to have it's desired effect cause almost instantly he started looking like Mr. Potato Head Man. The room got brighter but smaller and I felt I was swimming in my own thoughts. He got up and headed towards the stairs that he bought me down. I was out before he was even out of my sight.

Chapter 2

About One Year Earlier

"*E*noch I don't really feel comfortable doing this!" Karter stated in an attempt to get Enoch to back off.

"Bitch what the fuck you mean you don't feel comfortable doing it?" Screamed Enoch.

He was amped up off the blow he had been ingesting like a madman, not feeling Karters reluctance to play her role in his next caper. As far as Enoch was concerned, Karter was more than his ride or die bitch, she was also his property. She was either with him or against him, and at this moment she seemed to be leaning towards being against him.

His blood was starting to boil due to his frustrations as well as the effects of the alcohol mixed with the cocaine he was consuming. He took a swallow of the Bombay Sapphire Gin he was drinking, giving himself a moment to calm down and rethink his approach.

"Look, Randy already gave you the okay to make a guest appearance dancing at his club." Enoch stated as calmly as possible.

"With your looks mixed with the added weight you have put on in all the right places, there is no way Jokers fat ass will pass up the chance to snatch up the new girl on the scene. Your naiveté and presumed innocence will be your ace in the hole."

After Enoch finished speaking this time, the wheels in Karters' head were turning fast, already thinking of a way to punch holes in Enoch's plan.

"Okay, say it all works out as you say, and he takes me to his house. What am I to do if this fat muthafucka forces himself on me before you have a chance to get there? He could hurt me or my baby!" Enoch had heard enough. He was tired of the back and forth so he went full guerilla mode.

"Bitch fuck that baby! We getting rid of that muthafucka anyway! And I ain't trying to hear shit about no muthafucka forcing themselves on you as many times as you done already tricked that pussy off for the cause. Bitch boss up and quit playing with me!"

Enoch's last remarks were like a gut punch to Karter. Her last strands of dignity and respect left her body like an expelled breath. She had once again been defeated and decided then and there that she had no more strength for resistance.

She snatched the bottle of gin off the table and took a long pull, downing it like it was water. The liquor burned her insides going down but she was numb to its effects. She slammed the bottle down on the table, snatched the rolled up $100 bill out of Enoch's hand, and snorted up half the line he had separated out on the table he was sitting at.

Enoch sat there and looked at Karter like she was crazy. He smiled acknowledging his victory over her. He took the $100 bill back from her fingers as Karter stood there attempting to gain her bearings. He snorted up the rest of the coke on the table, and started from the top of the plan he had devised for their next caper...

Chapter 3

Karter was up on the stage doing her best exotic dancer impression. The thong she had on was being totally swallowed by her ample ass. She was on her hands and knees, bouncing her ass cheeks, like she had saw multiple other dancers do that graced the stage before her. To the trained eye it wasn't hard to tell that she was a novice, which was a real turn on for all the regulars. Nothing better than a fresh piece of ass to make men on the hunt go crazy.

Money was being thrown at Karter by the fist full, but not by her intended target. Joker was in the club in his regular booth giving the stage his full attention. He was a 300 pound plus Mexican kingpin, who felt he didn't have to move for anybody, especially some stripper who didn't know how to make her ass cheeks clap. Still he kept an eagles eye on her, he also surveyed the club in an attempt to see if she may have had a sponsor. It wouldn't be the first time he witnessed some young girl tricked into the life by a scumbag.

If this wasn't the case and she was working on her own, then she was the perfect type to fill his appetite.

Fucking with him could change her life instantly no more dancing at strip clubs for chump change. He was sure she was here for the money, probably for tuition or to support an expensive lifestyle. When her set was over Joker didn't waste any time sending one of his two goons to the dressing room to deliver his summons. He was intrigued by the new girl and wanted to pick her brain to see where she was at.

Randy the club owner already knew how Joker got down so him or his people never got any flack for working behind the scenes. Joker spent enough money at this establishment to own the place and he acted as if he did. Randy was up in his office watching and waiting. He knew Joker to be a creature of habit and knew the new flesh would pique his interest. He watched from his perch as one of Jokers goons headed towards one of the dressing rooms as soon as Karter left the stage.

He kept watch long enough to see him return with Karter trailing, posture looking as she if she was nervous and unsure of herself. He saw them converse for a second to get past the introduction phase. Karter got up and began to give Joker a lap dance, which told him that the hook had been set. From his spot overlooking the club he could see the look of pure bliss on Jokers face, and from past experiences he knew that the lap dance would never be enough to satisfy his hunger.

Randy picked up the phone from his desk and dialed a number. The line didn't finish it's first ring before it was answered with an "Uh Huh!" "Shouldn't be long now." Was all Randy said in return before hanging up the phone. His job was done now. The ball was out of his court. He hated doing this to such a great customer but lump sums beat crumbs every day of the week.

****

Everything was going as planned. After the initial introduction Karter had hit it off with Joker and was now riding with him in the back of his Cadillac Escalade. They were being chauffeured by Jokers goons, the driver being the same one had who came and got Karter from the dressing room. His partner was in the passenger seat twisted, head lolling back and forth with each turn the vehicle made. When the driver asked Joker where they were headed Joker informed him that he was to take them to the house.

The driver not really believing he had heard correctly asked Joker was he sure only to hear, "Fuck yeah I'm sure!" While they were riding Joker made sure he kept her attention so she could not get a sense as to where they were going. He had already taken her IPhone and powered it off as soon as they got in the truck. Karter and Enoch had both anticipated something like this happening and prepared for it.

She was wearing the newest Apple watch on her wrist equipped with a GPS tracker.

It wasn't hard for Karter to play her role and give Joker her undivided attention. He was paid, attentive, and wasn't hard to look at if you weren't repulsed by his weight. He also dressed nice, smelled nice, and was very respectful considering the circumstances. Karter was intrigued by how easily they got along as well as how open and vulnerable he seemed. He seemed to be driven, educated, but lacking confidence.

She played her role of being honestly interested in him like an Oscar winning actress. The truck after having made a million twists and turns stopped abruptly. Joker patted her leg signaling for her to get out of the truck. She stepped out of the truck only to be met by one of Jokers goons. He had her stand with both arms out to her side while he patted her down. He took his slow sweet time going over every curve of her body as well as inside every groove.

Karter could tell that he was enjoying himself, but never let on that she cared or was paying attention. When he was done Karter had the chance to get a good look at the house they were at and was instantly impressed. She told herself that this guy had to be the real deal; no run of the mill dope boy here. As they approached the front door she noticed a camera there looking down on them as well as a ring doorbell.

14

Karter started to feel overwhelmed and anxious. She no longer felt it would be as easy as Enoch explained to pull this lick off.

Her only consolation was that both Goons rode off in the Escalade after her and Joker were safely inside. Upon entering the foyer Joker instructed Karter to kick off her shoes and remove her jacket. She was kinda apprehensive about removing her jacket due to the watch on her wrist, but she did so quickly so she wouldn't bring any suspicion to herself. She noticed him looking at her wrist in a peculiar way, but just played it off waiting for further instructions.

"Follow me." Joker said before walking off through the house. As Karter entered the front room and her feet touched the plush carpet, she was taken aback by how lavish the furnishings were. There were paintings on the wall that seemed to have cost more than the house itself. The furnishings were ultra-modern and seemingly expensive. Joker just stood in the middle of the room looking at her with a knowing grin on his face.

He was breaking all his rules bringing her here and was satisfied with her reaction. "The paintings as well as some of the furnishings belonged to my father. I have never had anyone here who seemed to appreciate it all. I wasn't sure you would either, but it seems like you are amazed by it all." Karter couldn't help but ask, "What does your father do to be able to afford things like this?"

Joker turned to look at one of the paintings before on the wall before answering. "My father is dead and gone now, but the answer to your question is everything." Joker replied. "Everything sure looks as if it pays well." Karter said, her words filled with admiration. Amused by her last remark Joker just stood there smiling.

It took a moment before he replied. "Yeah well if things go like I hope them to, maybe I can do a little bit of everything with you. We can discuss the pay later." Hearing this brought Karter back to her senses and the job at hand. She had almost lost her edge due to the calm, caring, trusting nature of Joker. She had to be careful or chance losing herself in this man's world. She made a mental note to stay focused and get to the real reason why she was here. She had to get a lay of the land so she could have things prepared for Enoch's planned arrival...

Chapter 4

*E*noch was driving through the Kansas City streets like a madman trying to reach his destination. He was amped up and got like this whenever it was time to lash a muthafucka. He was riding to, "*One up top*" by Mozzy on repeat, and was in the zone ready to put in work. The Dodge Challenger he was driving was stolen and equipped with a faulty Kansas temp tag. He was constantly checking his IPhone, tracking Karter's location through her phone as well as her watch.

He could see the location on her watch wasn't moving unlike the one on her phone. He didn't really like the way technology worked now days; it wouldn't allow you to hide. Right now this fact seemed to be working in his favor so he accepted all it had to offer gratefully. The locator on Karter's phone was motionless at the moment also, which wasn't a surprise. He was sure that it was inside of the Cadillac Escalade about five cars ahead.

They were now at the light on Main St after exiting 71 South. Enoch had made it up in his mind that the only way he would ever get close to the house Karter was at, would be through the cover of the "Goons" Joker had with him everywhere he went. He had already rode past the house Karter was inside of, and could see that there would be no way to force entry without first getting killed or going to jail. He wasn't open to either one of these options so he planned to use the two Goons as his passkey.

Randy was the first to refer to these two as Goons. He could keep doing that if he wanted to but after doing his own homework on the Intel Randy gave him, Enoch found these two to be the real deal. It wasn't a coincidence that they were being paid to protect one of the Midwest's biggest suppliers of cocaine and methamphetamines. They were all said to be affiliates of "LA Emme" aka "Mexican Mafia."

Through past dealings, Enoch knew them to be vicious, violent, and very efficient. Randy confirmed that this was true about these two also, but only during work hours. When these two got the chance to party, one of them always took his turn to overindulge. They partied and drank just as efficiently, alternating between the two for who gets their chance to go overboard.

Enoch was expecting the passenger seat of the Escalade to be occupied by "Goon #2" the over indulger. The truck made a right turn onto Main St, heading west. Enoch was now only two cars back after having made the turn with them. He was shadowing their every move. He saw the brake lights light up before the truck made a turn into the parking lot of an all-night eatery called the Waffle House.

Enoch knew this was his chance, due to the fact that this restaurant didn't have a drive through window. As he rode past he noticed only one person get out of the truck and head into the Waffle House. He was talking on his cellphone not appearing to be in any hurry at all. Enoch continued to drive up the street about a half block before making a U-Turn. He drove to some apartments down the street, parked his car, got out, and hastily made his way back to where the truck was parked.

He had his black hoodie pulled low lessening the chances of him being identified. He knew from past experiences that shit could get out of hand and go bad at any moment. He could see the tailgate of the Escalade as he was making his way through the neighboring businesses parking lots. To his luck each lot was slightly up the hill from the next, allowing him the chance to come up from behind without being seen. To Enoch everything about this lash seemed right, as if it was meant to be.

Looking at his own Apple Watch he saw that only about eight minutes had passed since he first saw dude step out of the truck and walk into the restaurant. Every time he had eaten here it took a least a couple of minutes more than that to receive his order, whether he was dining in or taking it to go. He was now coming up the last incline right behind the truck. He stayed very low to the grass, moving forward in an alligator crawl. He finally made it to his planned destination.

After laying in the grass for a moment he heard what sounded like footsteps on the pavement approaching the trucks position. When he felt that the steps he heard were close enough he popped up like jack-in-the-box, brandishing his Carbine-15 equipped with a beta mag. Jokers Goon instantly knew this was serious business, and threw his hands in the air, after dropping his food and drinks to the ground. Enoch could tell he was trying to see past the hoodie and get a good look at his face. Enoch barked out orders with authority, "Hands down to your sides and walk towards me slowly!"

After the Goon complied, Enoch forced him to his knees and made him place his head on the rear passenger door of the Escalade. He jammed the muzzle of the Carbine-15 to the back of the Goons head and told him, "Move or make a sound and I will let this muthafucka rearrange your thoughts." Enoch proceeded to frisk the man and removed two Beretta 9mms, a wad of cash, a baggie containing what appeared to be meth, and the key fob to the truck.

The Goon finally worked up some nerve to speak,

"Puta if you were smart you would take what you have and run!"

"Run?" Enoch asked with a chuckle. "Only place I plan to run is through you, your boss, and everything y'all think y'all have going on! Now keep your forehead on this door and put your hands behind your back!" Enoch then put zip ties on the Goons hands locking them behind his back. "Now I want you to get to your feet very slowly."

The Goons weight plus the fact that his hands were behind his back made it hard for him to comply. Enoch grabbed his arm, jerking him to his feet after the Goon had managed to make it to one knee. His head bumped into the door in the process, making a noise Enoch could have lived without. Enoch unlocked the doors with the key, fob reached around the Goon and opened the back door. "Pop, pop, pop, pop!" Enoch instantly returned fire towards the front passenger seat before falling back on his back, waiting to see what would happen next.

In a split second he was back on his feet. He noticed Goon #1 slumped into the backseat head first, in a standing position. Enoch ordered whoever it was in the front seat of the truck to throw out their weapon and crawl out through the back seat. His orders went unanswered or complied too. Enoch realizing that it was a now or never situation, took a chance and looked through the backdoor towards the front seat.

He noticed Goon #2 was laying slumped on the dashboard, leaking from multiple gunshot wounds to the back and neck area. Enoch hurriedly lifted Goon #1 into the backseat, hopped into the driver's seat and tore out of the parking lot into the night's traffic at a high rate of speed. He turned onto Highway 71 headed straight to the house he knew Karter was at. His Carbine-15 had made gruesome mess of Goon #2.

Riding with two bodies had him rattled, but he was comforted by the fact that the Escalade was equipped with limo tint windows. Shit wasn't going as he had planned, but he felt that he was still in a good position to improvise. Enoch had made it safely to the house and backed the Escalade into the driveway. He knew there was no way he could get inside now, but he was hoping somebody especially Joker would eventually come out.

He sat there hoping none of the neighbors got nosey and called the police. He had no way to contact Karter who he knew was inside. He couldn't take the chance of trying to walkie her on the watch. He had found her phone inside the console powered off. He had also found another wad of cash inside the pockets of Goon #2. The gun Goon #2 had used to knock his own partner brains out with was lying on the floorboards, and Enoch decided that there was no use picking it up. Seeing that this was as far as he would get for the moment, Enoch let his seat back and waited for what would happen next...

Chapter 5

*K*arter could tell that Joker was honestly feeling her and she planned to take full advantage of that fact. She knew what she was here to do and couldn't allow herself to get caught up in his flattery, although it was hard for her not to. Joker was polite, he asked her questions about her goals and dreams and really listened with interest. He constantly complimented her on her beauty and her banging ass body.

He gave her his undivided attention, which was something Enoch never had done before. While Joker and Karter continued to converse and get more comfortable with each other, she noticed him getting more and more relaxed. To Karter this felt like a good, as well as, a bad thing. He was starting to let his guard down which was causing her to become a little anxious.

She wasn't sure how much longer her charm and wit would hold him off. Sooner or later he would want to do more than just talk. Karter's experience with men led her to believe all men only wanted one thing, especially ones like Joker. They had that major paper and felt that everything they came in contact with had a price tag, which in turn meant it could be bought.

If it couldn't be bought, then they took what they were after. Karter knew that Joker wanted to get between her legs. She felt he would probably take it if she didn't give it up, regardless of how nice and respectful he was. Karter was sitting on plush couch that matched the decor of Jokers bedroom. Everything in the house was elegant, expensive, and grand. The bedroom more so than everywhere else.

Joker was at the mini bar in the process of fixing them their third round of drinks. Karter never took her eyes off of his hands as he poured their drinks straight over ice. He walked over and handed her one of the drinks, and she downed half of it in one gulp. She felt she needed an extra buzz in order to do what she knew was sure she would end up having to do.

What she wished she had was a line or two, but she wouldn't risk relinquishing her position by asking Joker if he had any coke. As they sat there on the couch, talking, and sipping; Joker finally made his move. He placed one of his large hands on Karters thigh and started to rub it in circular motions. She kept sipping her drink, eyes locked with his, while she allowed him to continue on.

She needed to drown out her thoughts, so she kept telling herself it would just be sex. Joker was now kissing on Karter's neck and ear, while groping and feeling all over her body. Karter briefly thought of her pregnancy wishing this was a perfect world and that she could keep her baby. Jokers hand was now all the way up the inside of Karter's thigh, toying with the area by her pussy.

He told her to stand up and remove her pants, which she did with no hesitation. She sat back down on the couch and knew what was next. Joker pushed her thong to the side and slowly pushed two fingers into Karter's pussy. She took a deep breath before joining in on the foreplay. She cocked her legs open wider and started to rub and kiss on Joker also.

This excited him which caused him to start finger fucking her with reckless abandon. She stood up causing him to stop, and placed one leg over his lap and straddled him. She wondered what was Enoch doing as well as what was taking him so long. She kept hope alive that she wouldn't have to go through with completing the act, but it didn't seem as if luck was on her side.

Although she was wet and ready, she was still reluctant to go any further. She began to lick and suck on Jokers neck and ears as he was now finger fucking her from the back. She couldn't help but to moan as she grinded her pussy back on his thick fingers. Joker lifted her shirt and bra then put half of her right breast in his mouth. This pushed Karter past the point of no return. She stood up and made her way over to the California King Size Bed. She stripped the rest of her clothes off and stood there naked.

Her body was banging, perky B cups, slim waist, flat stomach, and a fat round ass. Her face was very easy on the eyes, set off by her caramel colored skin. Joker just sat there on the couch admiring her beauty as she paraded around the room, giving him a show. Joker sat and finished his drink, then told himself that he was tired of the games. He stood up, stripped down bare ass and walked over to Karter. He grabbed her in an embrace, and started to kiss and rub all over her.

Very passionately he handled her gently yet firm. His weight and size wasn't a hindrance to him at all which was apparent by the way he tossed and flipped Karter around the bed. Karter was now laying on her back while Joker was in between her legs sucking and licking her pussy like it was his last meal. Karter's whole body went into convulsions after about five minutes of the fire head Joker was delivering. He was a fucking pro, alternation from sucking her clit to fucking her with his tongue.

After about another ten minutes Karter was grabbing his head, begging him to stop. She had cum in his mouth twice and he just kept on going like the Energizer Bunny. It was like he was focused on seeing how far he could take her. Karter's mind was blown, this man was nothing like what she was used too. Her guards were down and she was now all in.

Joker finally came up for air, planting kisses on Karter's body making his way up to her titties.

Karter just laid there attempting to catch her breath. She was super worked up and her body was shaking like the aftershocks after an earthquake. While he had one of her titties in his mouth he took his dick and played with her pussy with the tip. This was the straw that broke the camel's back, causing Karter let out the loudest moan she could ever remember, while thrusting her pussy towards Jokers dick. No more reservations, she wanted all he was willing to give.

Joker stuck his tongue halfway down Karter's throat as he guided his dick into her pussy. After seeing how wet and warm Karter's pussy was he wasted no time pushing all the way in to the hilt. To Joker, Karter's pussy was just as good as it tasted. He slowly went in and out, as deep as possible, pausing after every thrust. Joker was taking his time to keep from cumin, however he wasn't sure he could keep it from happening.

Karter felt like Joker had single handedly killed the myth of the stereotype. He was well endowed and filling her every groove, touching all the spots needed touched. She was enjoying this and would keep doing so as long as it lasted. She justified her actions with the thought of how bad Enoch had treated her over they time they had been involved. The loving she was getting now made her wonder what else had she been missing out on fucking with Enoch. Jokers body started to convulse and shake instantly snapping Karter back to reality.

He kept pumping causing Karter to cum also. He rolled off of her, laying on his back, attempting to catch his breath. They were done and Karter was just lying there, ass wet with cum, trying to figure out what to do next.

The fairytale was over and it was now time to get back into jack mode. She starting thinking of a way to get Joker out of the room so she could attempt to walkie Enoch with her Apple Watch. She rolled over on her side, started stroking Jokers stomach before saying,

"All that good loving has made me build up an appetite. Do you have anything here we can eat?" Joker finally catching his breath just looked over at Karter and smiled. Karter looked right back into his eyes, without breaking contact, delivering an even bigger smile of her own.

"You are too beautiful to starve. I'll contact Rico and have them bring us something to replenish our energy. For now, there is bottled water and juices in the mini bar." Joker told her.

This was not what she wanted to hear, but didn't allow her face to show it. She just got up and walked her naked ass over to the bar and got a bottled water.

While she was doing so Joker picked up one of his cellphones and called his goons Karter could tell he was getting no answer due to the look in his face as well as the aggressive manner in which he kept redialing. She walked back over and sat on the bed.

"Something wrong?" she asked him.

Joker acted as if he didn't hear her as he kept hitting the button on his phone to redial the number he was trying to reach his goons on; cursing every time his call went unanswered. He jumped up from the bed, grabbed the remote control off the bedside stand and turned on the television that was mounted on the wall. Karter just watches with feigned concern on her face as he stared at the screen which seemed to be hooked up to his surveillance system. The television was showing nine different camera feeds which were placed at different spots throughout the property.

Joker apparently saw something that needed his immediate attention because he quickly dressed in a hooded sweat suit, told Karter he would be right back, and headed straight out the door. Karter just sat there on the edge of the bed pondering her next move. She got up to look at the monitor on the wall wondering what it was Joker saw that made him react so disturbed. Not knowing the layout of the property left her at a disadvantage to notice what was amiss, but she did notice that the Escalade had made its way back and was sitting in the driveway. She immediately took her watch off airplane mode and attempted to contact Enoch.

When she got no response, she ran around the room, grabbing her clothes off the floor, putting them on. Her instincts were telling her she needed to be ready for whatever may be going on. When she felt she had recovered everything she returned to the monitor, hoping to see something that would help her get a feel for what was going on. This time she could she that Joker had made it out the door headed towards the driveway. She attempted to walkie Enoch twice more, still getting no response. She didn't know what was going on as she watched Joker walk up to the passenger side of the Escalade and reach for the door handle…

****

Joker had hurried out the door pissed. Mentally talking to himself he made his way towards the truck.

"These two muthafuckas are getting on my last nerve!" Is what he was telling himself. He was seriously considering having these two replaced by the organization. Good living was dulling their edge as well as causing them to become lax. He was in the driveway now, ready to rip into the two for sitting out in his driveway, apparently high and drunk.

He strolled right up to the driver's side of the truck and went to open the door, hoping it was unlocked. His objective was to catch them slipping, so it could be used as an infraction to have them replaced. To his dismay the doors were locked, causing the handle to snap back into place, due to the aggressive nature in which he tugged on it. What he didn't know was that he had just woke up the bear that was hibernating and that he already needed replacements for his goons...

Chapter 6

*E*noch was startled out of his sleep by the sound of the door handle popping. As he was trying to gather his bearings, he noticed a giant fist pounding on the window, instantly bringing him all the way back to reality. He couldn't believe his luck. If there was ever a thing as divine intervention, to him this was it. Here was his mark hand delivered to him on a platter. Telling himself that it was now or never, he sprang into action. He grabbed his Cabine-15 with one hand while simultaneously opening the door with the other hand.

He pushed the door open with all his might, causing Joker to lose his footing and fall flat on his ass. Before Joker could realize what was going on he was staring down the barrel of Enoch's Carbine-15. The gun itself was enough to make Joker lose his bowels. The voice coming from behind the mask sent chills down his spine. "Get up and move now!" Jokers mind went into survival mode as his brain started to compute the words being thrown at him like knives.

"Get your fat ass up and move now bitch!" Was what Joker heard when he finally came back around mentally. Joker hurriedly scrambled to his feet with the agility of an Olympic gymnast. "Move!" was the next order. Joker didn't waste any time walking towards the front door entrance to the house. Joker felt he could easily get this situation under control, he had already a contingency plan for times like this.

As he and Enoch crossed the threshold of the entrance Joker immediately started talking,

"Look amigo, I have money and drugs, enough to change your life. Just don't kill me please!"

Enoch was surveying the room they had just entered and was instantly impressed. He was thinking, *If dude is living like this then there is a good possibility I will come out of here a rich man.*

"What the fuck makes you think you can offer me what I already know I can take, whether it be your life or your money!" Enoch asked. "Lay your fat ass face down in the middle of that floor and put both of your hands behind your back."

Enoch pulled out zip ties and locked both of Jokers hands behind his back. It took three of them to do so being that Joker was so fat. Enoch also did the same to Jokers ankles. He then used zip ties to bound Jokers arms to his legs, leaving him in the middle of the floor looking like a Thanksgiving turkey. Now he felt he could search the house for Karter or anybody else that may be inside. While all this was going on Joker kept attempting to negotiate for his life.

Some of the things he allowed to slip out of his mouth were exactly what Enoch wanted to hear. Enoch wasn't really sure if he was attempting to negotiate or trying to alert someone. Enoch felt the circulation of the air in the room change, alerting him to a presence stirring. He instantly lifted his weapon aiming it towards the entrance to the hallway. He saw Karter standing there peeping around the corner, uncertain as to whether she should enter the room or wait for Enoch to come and get her.

Eye contact with him told her all she needed to know, "Don't Move! Who are you in this house with fat boy?" Enoch asked Joker.

"Nobody but my lady." Joker replied. "Please don't hurt us. I will give you whatever you want." Enoch was feeling shit was going better than planned. He felt he could get this done without having to kill Joker or blow Karter's cover. Less tracks for him to have to cover considering what he already had to clean up outside in the truck.

"All right." Enoch said. "Where is the money and drugs you are blabbing about?"

"Inside the safe." Joker answered immediately. He sounded relieved being that he could now see which direction this thing was going.

"Where is this lady of yours you speak of?" Enoch asked.

When Karter heard this the hairs on the back of her neck stood up. Her senses were warning her of what was to happen next. She hoped she was wrong but her stomach told her that she wasn't.

She pictured herself now playing a role that she never would have agreed to play. "Baby Girl Come out here!" Joker screamed. *Damn!* Karter thought to herself. She was uncomfortable not knowing how all of this was going to play out. She walked into the living room not surprised to see Enoch standing over Joker with his gun on him. As soon as her presence was noted Enoch started barking out orders.

"Bitch! Get over here and lay face down on this floor!" Karter did exactly as she was told. Enoch was roughing her up the whole time. He was extra rough with her as he trussed her up exactly as he had done Joker. He could tell by the appearance of her clothing that she had done more than converse with Joker all night.

His blood started to boil due to thoughts of Karter getting her freak on while he was out risking his life trying to gain entry to the house. It didn't help his mood any that Joker had referred to her as his girl. After he finished with Karter he got right back to business.

"Where is this money and dope? You better have enough of it if you and your girl plan to live through this!" Enoch asked Joker.

"It's in the safe, hidden behind my shoe rack, in the closet." Joker hurriedly responded. After hearing this Enoch decided that it was time to inspect the premises.

He rolled Joker and Karter onto their sides and zip tied them together in that position. Karter visibly showed her aggravation and expelled deep breath as Enoch did so. After he had their bonds secured, Enoch took off to search the house in hopes to find all it may be hiding. He was going through the house gun out in front of him, clearing each room as he went about his business. He came upon some stairs that led down to the garage.

Damn this boy got that cake! Enoch said to himself. In the three car garage was not only a brand new Metallic Gray Phantom, but there was also a Black Bentley Continental taking up damn near two of the carports. There was a giant T.V. room with multiple 70-inch screen monitors on the walls, a fully stocked bar equipped with a stripper pole, in the middle of a cul-de-sac of plush couches. Enoch was impressed by this alone without mentioning the game room filled with arcade games. Enoch knew he had found is golden egg and was excited.

T.Marie

He found the garage door opener for the empty carport and opened the garage. He hastily made his way to the Escalade, hopped in, hoping no nosey neighbors were paying any attention. The truck itself shouldn't cause any suspicion, but the nigga with the mask on would. He backed the truck into the garage and closed it, feeling better about his position. He jumped out, opened the rear passenger door and dragged the body of Goon#1 out by his legs.

The head of the body hit the floor of the garage, making a sound that made Enoch want to throw up. He wasn't prepared for the sound that blood, bone and brain makes when it hits the floor. Goon#1's head hitting the floor sounded like somebody dropped a trash bag full of wet oatmeal from about 10 feet high off the ground. Blood and brain fragments were leaving a messy trail on the polished marble floor of the garage as Enoch dragged it into the game room, leaving it in the middle of the floor once he got it there.

He returned to the truck and retrieved the body of Goon #2 doing the same thing with the body. After he was done with the two he retrieved Goon #2's Glock 9mm of the floorboard of the truck and left it with the bodies. He grabbed towels off the bar and cleaned the inside of the truck as best as he could. He had executed his body search of the house and secured his exit vehicle. Now knowing it was only him, Karter and Joker inside the house, he decided it was time to get what he came for.

He made his way back to the room where Joker and Karter laid in the middle of the floor trussed up like cattle waiting to be branded. Seeing them laid there like this brought an idea to Enochs mind. He turned and went to the kitchen. He grabbed a butcher knife out of block on the counter. He placed the knife blade first on the fire and left it there. He was hoping these preparations weren't needed, but he would rather be safe than sorry.

He returned to the room with Joker and mustering up all the menace possible said, "Aight fat ass! How am I supposed to get in this safe?"

"I will give you the combination." Joker answered, sounding relieved that things seemed to going in a way in which he was comfortable.

"WHAT'S TAKING YOU SO LONG?" Enoch asked Joker, while simultaneously kicking him in the face. The kick angered Joker as Enoch could tell by the venom dripping from every word coming out of Jokers mouth as he recited the combination.

"And what exactly am I to find when I get this safe open?" Enoch asked.

"Every dime I have to my name, 12 kilos of coke, and 6 pounds of 90% pure meth." Joker replied.

"No silent alarms or tricks?" was Enochs next question.

"No, No, No tricks at all! Take what's there, it's all yours! Just please don't kill us!" Joker told him. Karter was just lying there pissed for allowing herself to end up in this position. She could see that Enoch was going off script, and hated not knowing what was to happen next.

Joker had spoken up twice in defense of Karter while hogtied with a big ass gun in his face. This realization alone made upon Enoch's mind on how he was going to play this situation. Enoch left them there and went to Jokers room in search of the safe. He found the room he assumed to be Jokers, judging by the decor, and unmade bed.

The furnishings were dark mahogany. He saw the 70-inch screen television on the wall, which was showing all angles of the outside of the property from 9 different feeds. As he was making his way towards the closet, he saw a flash of color, that seemed to be out of place amongst the mahogany and dark color of the carpet. He didn't allow this to distract him as he continued on his mission. Walking into the closet left Enoch in awe. Joker had enough shoes on the wall to start his own shoe store.

He also had shelves and racks built matching the bedroom set and other furnishings. He had vintage, original, and custom makes of every sneaker imaginable. Enoch shook off the daze that came with his surprise at seeing all this. He made his way to the back wall, hit the latch, releasing the shelf that hid the safe. Enoch put in the combination on the numerical keypad and pulled the release lever...

****

Karter was now crying and acting hysterical. She was fighting the zip ties that had her bound to Joker. Joker was trying to calm her down, "Mi amor don't worry about a thing. This will be over soon and anything taken can be replaced. I promise to take you somewhere to make you forget all this ever happened. Just calm down and stop moving please?" The restraints were already cutting off his circulation, it didn't help any that he was also bent up like a pretzel. He was just as anxious as Karter to get out of the situation.

Joker was certain by now the masked man had found the stash, cause he could hear him moving back and forth down the hall to the garage. It had been at least ten minutes since he last left them there like that. As they say, "Just thinking of the devil invites him into your home." In walks the masked man with words Joker was not expecting to hear.

"Where is the rest of it fat ass?" Enoch asked him.

"I don't know what you are talking about." Joker replied nervously. "If you opened the safe, you should have found exactly what I said was there."

Enoch squatted down next to Jokers face, now holding the knife with the glowing red blade he had just retrieved from the fire. He held it next to Jokers face as he explained to him how he knew why there had to be more. He summed up that the safe was a little too neat and convenient for it to be everything. Nothing more than Enoch's intuition led him to believe this.

He felt that the safe was Jokers safety measure for a moment like the one they were in. The money itself was too clean and neat. The drugs themselves looked as if it hadn't been touched in ages. Everything fit in the safe a little too nice and snug. Too Enoch it seemed like this was Jokers sucka ransom, just enough for any would be robber to find and be happy with. Mostly with a bullseye on your back also, due to the instant change in your status and living conditions.

Taking the bait and spending it was a fast way to get killed, which was not why Enoch was there. Although, he had already loaded those things up in the Escalade as well as three trash bags filled with Jokers sneakers. Enoch was a sneaker head who happened to notice him and Joker wore the exact same size. This was the type of sign that told Enoch the shoes were meant to have. The order of the contents of the safe told him that Joker was holding out.

He laid the blade of the knife on Jokers face instantly searing flesh on contact. Joker jerked his head back in pain, but Enoch kept the applied pressure on the blade of the knife, ensuring he got his point across. Joker seemed to be getting the point judging by his pleas as well as curses. Enoch used this moment to tell Joker what conclusions he had come up with and wasn't leaving this house without the real payday. He also informed Joker on how they would spend the time together until he regained his memory.

Enoch took the knife off of Jokers face and cut the ties that bound him and Karter together. He then cut the ties that held Karter's hands to her feet, all the while Karter was still faking hysteria. She was doing such a good job Enoch couldn't tell if she was faking or not.

"How about I ask your girl if she knows where the real money is? Maybe she would like to have her chance to end this charade?" Enoch turned his interrogation towards Karter.

"Listen bitch! I am only going to ask you once. Where is what I came for?" Enoch felt that if Karter couldn't tell him anything then that was her ass, literally! Karter never broke her role as she screamed. She had no idea what he was talking about. Enoch was livid and past thinking rational. His way of thinking was the only way of thinking.

He was now convinced that Karter had spent more time through the night enjoying herself than accomplishing what she was sent here to do. Even though he would have never found this house without her, Enoch was in a rage due to his perceptions of how Karter must have spent her time there with Joker. "One of you will talk before I leave here!" Enoch said as he took the knife and started to cut the leggings Karter was wearing. He began from the small of her back to her crotch area. It was no surprise to him that Karter's whole ass was now exposed, due to the fact that she was panty less. He snatched her up roughly to her knees, undid the front of his pants, and stroked his dick to erection.

Once he was ready he spat a gob of spit into his palm, applied to the tip of his dick, and pushed it into Karter's ass to the hilt. Karter let out a scream like she was being killed. Her screams didn't faze Enoch as he kept pumping like a dog in heat. He asked both of them simultaneously. "Where is what I came for?" Joker was now really pissed. He wanted to murder the masked man in the worst way possible.

He wanted the man out of his home, but couldn't give him all of what he was now convinced he was there for without signing his own death warrant. Just when Karter's screams were starting to really get to Joker; they stopped cause the masked man had stopped pumping. Enoch was getting tired of hearing

Karter's screams so he dug into his pocket, and pulled out the article that had caught his attention earlier while in Jokers bedroom. It was a pair of pink see through panties, that he was sure Karter was wearing before she left to go to the strip club.

He took the panties, shoved them into Karter's mouth, then continued his sexual assault on her asshole. Karter saw the flash of pink cross before her eyes, before the panties were stuffed into her mouth, and knew she was in for it. In her haste to get dressed she failed to locate the underwear. She knew that this one mistake alone upset the balance of how things were supposed to play out.

She now just accepted the abuse to her ass, hoping that things wouldn't get worse, but her knowing Enoch she doubted it. The muffled sounds of Karter's cries mixed with the sound of slapping flesh caused Joker to have an epiphany. In the trunk of his Phantom could be the key to saving his life. He had a duffle bag full of cash, as well as 3 pounds of meth from his last drop. He wanted to have his Goons kick Freddy's ass for not having the full amount of cash for his order. Having to make two trips with product was a "No No!"

He ended up taxing Freddy extra for what he could purchase, and left him with a stern warning. He was now feeling blessed that he never returned everything to the safe house. Hopefully its contents would be enough that he had everything that he came for. Joker had just finished his thoughts almost simultaneously as the sound of slapping skin. Grimacing through the pain caused by his burnt and blistered jaw, he spat out, "In the trunk of the Phantom!"

"What was that?" Enoch asked.

"Keys on the top of the dresser! In the trunk of the Phantom!" screamed Joker.

"Aw yeah?" Enough roughly snatched the panties out of Karter's mouth, and wiped blood, cum, and feces off his dick with them. When he finished he took the panties and shoved them inside of Jokers mouth.

Enoch chuckled before saying, "Here's a little something to snack on from me and your girl."

He then got up, grabbed his gun, and went to find what was supposed to be in the trunk of the Phantom. He entered the bedroom and the keys were right there where Joker said they would be. There was also some nice pieces of jewelry Enoch had failed to notice in his haste to get to the safe. He wished he had the time as well as the manpower to really ransack the house. He was sure he would find a king's ransom. Enoch had already made up in his mind that whatever was in the trunk would have to be enough, cause he was outta there with whatever it was.

He made his way to the garage and hit the trunk pop on the Phantom key fob. Inside the trunk was a large duffle bag that immediately grabbed Enoch's attention. He unzipped it and saw large knots of circulated cash as well as what appeared to be crystal meth. He zipped it back satisfied and ready to get the fuck outta here. He loaded the duffle bag into the Escalade with the rest of his take. He did a once over of the outside of the vehicle. Satisfied with what he saw, he hopped into the driver's seat, hit the garage door opener, and rode off into his new life. Hoping all the while that he would make it to his destination safely...

Chapter 7

*E*noch was driving along Highway 71 as cautious as possible, trying to reach his destination without any issues. He was riding with the score of his life and wasn't looking to lose it before he had the chance to count it. He exited the highway on Main Street nervous as fuck. He wasn't sure if the police were looking for the Black Escalade he was now behind the wheel of. Last night's shooting involving the vehicle could be all over the bulletins.

He made a left onto Main St. and headed for the apartment complex his Challenger was left parked at. Holding his breath, the whole time, he made the short journey, with no mishaps. It was early and there wasn't much traffic which made him uneasy. He didn't want to be noticed as he switched vehicles but this was a chance he had to take. With his hood pulled down to his eyebrows, he hopped out, and quickly put the bags taken from Jokers house in the trunk of the Challenger.

It crossed Enoch's mind how fucked up it would be to be identified, due to him having to make multiple trips to the Escalade, cause of his love for sneakers. He told himself, "It is what it is!" as he closed the trunk and hopped into the driver's seat, and rode off into his new life.

"One up top" was still playing through the speakers. He rapped the words along with Mozzy as he turned onto the highway. "Suckas talk tough and then fall back, if that ain't a bitch nigga what you call that? Riding with the illest and we all strapped. Truthfully; I am just being honest. That was all facts!" Enoch was feeling himself as the music calmed his nerves. He played the previous night's events over in his mind, looking for mistakes he may have made. He knew he would need to give Randy his cut for the good information. He would make that a top priority once he secured himself and the score.

He had to come up with a safe place to go. He settled on finding a motel somewhere he wouldn't be noticed. He also had to make sure it wouldn't be a place that would bring unwanted attention to him. He exited the highway on 95th St. and got right back on it headed south. He felt that the Belton Inn served his needs perfectly. Easy access to the highway, as well as the rooms being accessible from the parking lot. He thought of Karter for a brief moment. He felt that he had left her in a position where she should make it out okay, if not, he no

longer needed her anyway.

He was convinced he had really pulled off the heist alone. She was getting her pussy busted open while he damn near lost his life trying to gain entry to Jokers crib. If Joker wanted to consider her his girl, then apparently they connected in more ways than one. His thoughts cleared when he entered the Belton Inn parking lot. He went inside, paid for two rooms that connected from the inside.

He backed into one of the parking spots, right in front of one of the rooms he rented. He got out the car, and quickly went inside one of the rooms and unlocked the door that adjoined the two. He came out hoping nobody saw him. He grabbed the bags from the trunk and entered the other room with them. Enoch's heart was racing. He had gotten away with the biggest lash him and Karter had ever come across. He thought of Karter, her not being there with him kind of had him fucked up.

He couldn't be sorry for how things played out. If Goon #2 had of been a better shot, then he would be dead. The way Joker was pleading for Karter's safety infuriated him, but it also lead him to believe that she should come out of the situation okay. If so she was sure to be pissed about two things him leaving her as well as him fucking her in her ass like that. Out of all the time they had been fucking around, she wouldn't even let him go near her asshole. Enoch chuckled at the thought as he unlocked the door and carried his score into the other room.

He felt just a little safer believing that anyone who may have happen to see him enter would believe that he was in the other room. He dumped both bags onto the bed and took a moment to admire the look of the cash mixed with the drugs laying on the bed. He wasn't sure what to do with the meth cause he didn't know anybody that fucked with it. He would cross that bridge when he got to it. Right now he wanted to crack the seal on one of the bricks of cocaine, snort a few lines, and then get to counting this paper.

He first took off his Apple watch, snatched off both bands and flushed it down the toilet. He wasn't taking any chances on being tracked down. He grabbed one of the bricks off the bed, and tore into its wrapping with his teeth. He opened it just enough to get him something out to toot. After accomplishing this task, he was high as fuck and ready to get down to business. He started with the money that was in the bag from the Phantom. It was in rubber band bundles, so he broke one open and got to it.

After going through three of them he had counted out 15 thousand dollars, so he assumed that each bundle had 5 thousand dollars each. There were forty of these stacks so he calculated the bundles to add up to 200 thousand dollars. He grabbed one of the stacks from the safe and counted it. It was one hundred, hundred dollar bills, all seeming to be new. With there being 25 of these Enoch could see that he had 450 thousand dollars in front of him.

He wasn't fucking with the stacks. He felt that they could maybe be traced back to him in some way. He was rich from the cash alone, not even mentioning what he took from the pockets of Jokers Goons. He was real turnt up off the coke and was too impatient to count all the money to get a final tally. He eyed the pieces of jewelry on the bed and picked them up piece by piece, putting them all on. There were two, what he believed to be, platinum chains judging by their weight.

One large Cuban Link with diamonds in each link and a solid rope with a diamond encrusted Jesus Piece. Three rings with multiple various sized diamonds, as well as a bracelet that looked as if it cost more than all the other pieces together. It was about 4 inches wide with invisible set princess cut diamonds going around the whole thing. Enoch tried on the rings, but they were way too big for his fingers, so he just put them in his pocket. He took the meth as well as the bricks and placed them back in one of the bags.

He then took all of the money accept for what he took off of the Goon's and twenty of the 5 thousand dollar bundles and scooted it off the bed into the other bag. He placed them both in the cabinet, under the sink, in the bathroom. He snatched the trash bag out of the garbage can and placed the other cash as well as the brick he kept out in it. He cleaned the excess coke off the table, grabbed his guns, and went back to the other room, shutting both doors behind him.

When he got to the other room he snatched the trash bag out of the can and placed the Nike boots he was wearing in it. He was sure blood traces had to be on them, so getting rid of them was a top priority. He rifled through one of the trash bags full of sneakers from Jokers crib, and settled on a vintage pair of Jordan 3's. After putting them on, he grabbed his keys and the rest of his things and headed back to his Challenger.

Chapter 8

*K*ater laid on the floor hurting, ass wet with blood and Enoch's semen. She was still trussed up. Her last hope went out the window when she heard what sounded like the garage door opening and closing then total silence. Her mind went into overdrive, knowing that it was now up to her to come out of this ordeal alive. She struggled against her bonds, only hurting her wrist and ankles in the process.

She rolled over onto her back and felt something hard and cold on her exposed ass cheeks. Instantly she knew that it had to be the knife Enoch had used to burn Jokers face and cut through her pants. Just thinking about Enoch had her pissed, but she put those feelings aside being that they couldn't help her now. She went into survival mode. She scooched down attempting to grab the handle of the knife. She pricked her thumb on the blade and didn't get the least bit discouraged.

She finally got the handle of the knife in her hands, and then had to make a decision on if she was going to try to free herself or Joker first. Joker saw Karter moving with a purpose and asked her with a voice filled with concern what she was doing. She turned on her side showing him the knife in her hands. Joker had already managed to spit Karter's dirty cum stained, bloody panties out of his mouth that Enoch had used to gag him.

As soon as he saw the knife, he told Karter to try to get it to his mouth so he could attempt to cut her bonds free. When Karter heard this she felt better about her chances of making it out alive. She maneuvered herself into position to get the handle into Jokers mouth. On the first attempt she accidentally rubbed across the raw wound left on Jokers face by the hot blade of the knife. Joker winced and let out a curse, but managed to get the knife on the second attempt.

He was able to hold the knife in position to cut Karter's' hands free. After her hands were free, Karter cut all of Jokers bonds before freeing her feet. She was hoping this act of consideration would earn her brownie points. As soon as all their bonds were free, they just laid there for about five minutes. She was waiting to see what he would do when all the feeling returned to his limbs.

After what seemed like a long ass time he finally asked was she okay. Karter instantly burst into tears, playing her last ace in the hole. "Baby girl! Please don't cry." Joker said in attempt to console her. "I will make everything alright. That bastard will suffer for this violation of you and my home! Believe that!" Joker said to her. "Now let me get up so I can make sure we are alone in this house and that everything is now safe and sound."

Karter just laid there and nodded her head that she understood. Joker got up and left the room, returning five minutes later talking on the phone, with a large towel in his hand. To Karter he no longer looked like the big teddy bear who had made love to her just hours ago. He now looked like a vicious polar bear, due to his angry mood and the ugly red blister starting to form on his face. He was spewing curses into the phone, alternating from Spanish to English.

"Just get the clean-up crew here now!" was the last thing he said before hanging up. After ending the call Joker kneeled down next to Karter and wiped the tears from her face. He kept uttering assurances that everything would be okay, as he wrapped the towel around her, while placing one arm under her legs, and the other under her back, lifting her in his arms like small child.

He carried her in his arms down the hall into the bathroom. He put her down on her feet and proceeded to undress her slowly and carefully. Karter was in a trance as she surveyed the opulence of the room. Gold fixtures on the sinks, the lighting, as well as on the trim around the walk in multi head shower. The whole room with its matching toiletry looked as if belonged in the grandest hotel ever built.

When he was done undressing her he picked Karter up and carried her to the extra-large hot tub that seemed to dwarf the room. He held her hand she stepped into the hot water topped by fragrant bubbles. Karter's muscles and joints instantly felt better as she sat down and laid her head back on one of the built in waterproof pillows. He sat on the edge of the tub and watched her for a moment, eyes showing satisfaction in her instant reaction to the ambiance. He left her there like that after he could tell that she had fallen asleep...

Chapter 9

Present Day

I woke up with a splitting headache as well as my dry mouth tasting like I had eaten a shit sandwich. I noticed that my hands were cuffed to a chain hanging from a pipe in the ceiling. I struggled against my bonds, succeeding in doing nothing but hurting my wrist, so I gave no effort. I didn't know where I was or how I had gotten here. I looked around at my surroundings and realized I was in some type of dirty basement or cellar.

My bladder felt as if it was about to burst due to my fear and anxiety. While I sat on this dirty ass mattress I continued to survey the room and noticed a bucket and a large bottle of water sitting at the foot of the mattress. With no other choice, I made my way over to the bucket, balanced myself over it, and relieved myself in it. Not only did I have to pee, but my bowels let go of a wet watery shit that had the foulest odor I ever remember coming from my body. I noticed that I didn't have any panties on and with no understanding as to why.

I didn't know where I was, how I had gotten in this position, or who put me in it. I tried my best to recollect my last memory and came up with nothing. After relieving myself, I tore a piece of my dress off, wet it with the water from the bottle, and wiped myself as best as I could. I then downed the rest of the water, wishing I had two more bottles just like it.

I wanted to attempt to explore my surroundings but the chain wouldn't allow me to go any further. Just getting this far and using the bucket as a toilet expended all my energy. I plopped back down on the mattress and winced soon as my head touched its surface. I reached behind my head and discovered a knot there the size of an egg. Just touching it made my eyes water.

I closed my eyes and attempted to think of how I ended up in this situation and why. My concentration was interrupted by the sound of footsteps coming down the stairs. A large man with a mask on walked into view and stood next to the mattress. He was dressed in dark pants and a dark colored long sleeve shirt. He had his face covered with a knit ski mask, and on his hands were latex gloves.

I just sat there chilled by the look of those dark colored eyes staring a hole right through me. He carried a bag from McDonald's, a large bottle of water, and an extension cord. He threw the bag at me then said" I thought you might be hungry. Just as he was saying this, I heard another voice from somewhere up the stairs say, "I don't know why you feeding that bitch! Fuck her! You should just let me kill her!" I wasn't certain but I felt that I had heard both voices before. My present state wouldn't allow me to concentrate enough to be sure.

He responded with a stern, "Shut the fuck up bitch and stop questioning my actions!" He looked at the bucket then turned his attention back to me. "I think you might want to eat that before she comes and takes it from you." I got up, used the wall as a backrest, and tore open the bag. There were two cheeseburgers with French fries, which I ate like it would be my last meal.

I drank half of the bottle of water and felt stuffed. My captor just stood there and watched the whole time, eyes filled with satisfaction. As soon as I was done he said, "You took something from me that I will have back, if you plan to leave this place with your life." I responded by telling him that I didn't know what he was talking about. And that he had the wrong person.

"Karter, how far did you expect to get in this life pretending that the world would never see you for what you are?" He continued on me. This question unnerved me, cause he had referred to me as what instead of who. I couldn't be sure what he meant by this, but it felt like he had dehumanized me in his mind.

Judging by the conditions in which he held me captive, I was almost sure that this was the case. I told him that I was a respectable, honest business woman, and had no idea what he was talking about. He bellowed out the most menacing laugh I had ever heard. "I was coming down here to tell you what it would cost you to obtain your freedom, but after hearing your bullshit I feel as if you need something that will help you think about who and what you really are."

With that being said he pulled a package containing a needle from his pocket, as well as a glass vial containing a clear liquid I was unfamiliar with. He had stuck the needle in the glass vial, pulling back on the needle, until it was full. After placing the vial back in his pocket, he uncurled the extension cord and stepped on the bed, closing the distance between us.

As he approached me I couldn't help but think that I had saw this scenario before. Before I had my chance to finish my thought, he roughly grabbed my arm, and tied the extension cord around my arm super tight. As soon as he found my vein, he stuck in the needle and pushed the plunger, forcing the needle to empty its contents into my veins.

I could have struggled, but I didn't in fear of causing him to do more damage than he already was. Whatever he had given me took effect immediately and I got an instant head rush. All of a sudden I was looking at a cartoon character, with a big ass head, standing over me. I slowly slumped down the wall, until I was on my back, staring at the ceiling.

I remember hearing him say something, but it sounded like jibber jabber to me. I honestly couldn't make out a word he was saying. My eyes were getting too heavy to keep open so I closed them. I saw a face that I would always remember yet never wanted to see again. With my last conscious thought, I asked the face, "Enoch! What are you doing here?"

Chapter 10

*E*noch was hype and moving down the highway at a good clip. He was in an elated state cause of his new found wealth. He had to get something to eat, dump the filthy sneakers, and get a new phone so he could network. He exited on Gregory and headed towards the landing mall. After a short drive he pulled into the BP on Troost.

Getting out the car he went in and paid for some gas, and purchased some backwoods. Afterwards he pumped his gas, and dumped the filthy sneakers in the gas station dumpster. He didn't really like being out in the open like this, but it was early, and he didn't expect to run into anybody he knew.

After pumping his gas, he headed to the McDonald's across the street. Pulling through the drive through he ordered a 10-piece chicken nugget meal with a large Hi-C orange drink. After paying for his meal with a $100 bill, he told the cashier to keep the change, headed across the street, to the Landing Mall parking lot, and sat and scarfed down his meal. After he was finished he went inside the mall to the Cricket store there he purchased two phones with car chargers.

Returning to his car he was focused on devising a plan what to do next. He plugged the phones in and first called Keisha. After the phone rang for what seemed like forever, he finally got an answer from a groggy voiced female, who didn't seem so happy about having to answer a call so early, from a foreign number.

"Who's this?" was how she answered.

"This Enoch." He replied.

Enoch?" she responded sounding puzzled as to why he was calling her phone, especially this early.

"Yeah! I need you to be up and ready. I am about 20 minutes away from you and it's very important that you have that muthafucka cleaned out by the time I get there!" Enoch knew how Sis ran her house. He knew that meant that anybody could be there from the night before. He was cool with Jay, her man, but he couldn't afford to have any other stragglers in his mix.

"Nigga what type of bullshit you on?" was Keisha's reply, although her tone had changed.

"Sis you know I wouldn't even ask if it wasn't real as well as profitable. I can't do all that on this phone. I just need you to trust me and do me this solid." He answered back.

"Aight I got you bro. Just make sure you don't bring no bullshit to my home." she told him sternly.

"Thanks Sis, but I already know better than that." replied Enoch. He hung up on the call, picked up the other phone and dialed Randy's number.

"Who dis?" was how Randy answered the phone. Enoch had a thought go through his mind about how ill-mannered everybody he fucked with was.

"The eagle has landed." Was all Enoch had to say.

"Aw yeah?" Randy replied. "Tonight at the agreed upon spot."

Was all Enoch said before ending the call. Enoch was moving on pure adrenaline. He was amped up off the fact that he was sure his life had changed for the better. Yeah, there was a little more work that must be put in, but the heavy lifting was over.

He started up the car, turned up his music, and got into traffic. As he was riding, he thought about Karter, wondering if he had done the right thing by leaving her. He was sure he hadn't done anything to compromise her. After those bodies had dropped there was no logical reason to make her a full accomplice. Jokers house had surveillance cameras along the outside perimeter. There was sure to be footage of her and Joker entering the residence together.

Leaving with her would only have forced his hand to leave Jokers fat ass stinking. He wasn't bothered by the thought of that. What bothered him was the fact that after only one night that fat muthafucka was extra protective of her, referring to her as his girl and all. Enoch made up his mind that the situation wasn't worth overanalyzing, since he got away with what he went in for.

He was focused on getting to Keisha's, whipping up this dope, and getting shit cracking. 12th St. was the perfect spot to start his takeover, and Sis was the perfect person to jumpstart the operation. She had been living down there forever, and knew everybody that was somebody. "Yeah shit would be aight." was Enoch's last thought on the matter, before making a turn onto Highway 71, headed north, to Keisha's spot...

Chapter 11

Enoch was making his way north on Highway 71, in an elated state, head bobbing to the music. He knew that it was a must that he gets rid out the Challenger, just in case someone may have saw him, and linked it to last night's events. He picked up one of his cellphones and dialed his young nigga Drako's number, after two rings he answered. "What it do?"

"What's up youngin?" replied Enoch.

"Who dis?" Drako asked not recognizing the voice or the number in his caller I.D.

"Dis Knock Knock!" Enoch said with a chuckle.

"Aw what's up cuzzin?" Drako replied.

"Aye nigga what I tell you about cuzzing me?"

Enoch said aggravated by being called cuzz. He had never rocked with the Crips and hated being called cuzz.

"My bad big homie. You know that I didn't mean any disrespect, it's just how I talk cu." Drako caught himself this time before letting the word slip out again. "See you got me checking myself and shit homie. What's good anyway?" Drako got straight to the point.

"I need a fresh whip!" Enoch always rode in stolies. He felt that since he wasn't stopping for the law anyway, there was no use in riding legit. Drako and his crew made a hustle out of stealing new cars from the Claycomo Ford factory as well as other dealerships.

"I got a brand new Mustang GT that has yet to even see the streets." Drako knew that hearing this would instantly make Enoch's mouth water. "I was waiting for my bro to come and slap that limo tint in this bitch. If you want to. you can come and get this muthafucka right now Big Homie." Drako explained to him.

"Hell yeah that sounds right upon my alley!" Enoch said hyped up by hearing the make and model. "I'm about five minutes away from you. I'll hit you when I am outside."

"Nigga we outside posted up in the back right now! Just pull right up into the backyard." Drako instructed him. "Word." said Enoch before ending the call.

Enoch exited on 39th St. and made his way east until he got to Olive St. He bust a left on Olive and made his way to their middle of the block where Drako stayed with his mother. Once there, he pulled into the driveway and proceeded all the way to the backyard.

Just like Drako said, him and about five of his crew were standing around in the backyard smoking. Enoch knew they were into other drugs as well, so there was no telling what they may have been under the influence of. It amazed Enoch how much things had changed since he was young. When he was these young niggas age he was selling dope and shooting hoops. Putting any type of drug up your nose was a No-No.

Drako walked up to the passenger side door, opened it, and hopped right in, with a backwood blunt hanging from his lips. Enoch was just sitting there admiring the Mustang. He was telling himself, stolen or not he couldn't wait to get behind the wheel of that bitch.

"What's good Big Homie?" Drako said as he was closing the door.

"Shit! Nothing really My Nigga, just have urgent business to get to."

"Word! That's what's up! Drako replied.

"I see that muthafucka is my color and everything. What you want for it?" Enoch asked him.

"I really already had other plans for it, but you can get it if the price is right." Drako was now sitting there hoping Enoch didn't attempt to low ball him.

"Check it!" Enoch said. "I'll give you $2,500 and I'll let you have this Challenger. Drako was now looking the car over searching for flaws that weren't there.

"What's wrong with it Homie?" Drako asked wondering why Enoch would be willing to give up cash as well as a perfectly good car.

"There's nothing wrong with it." Enoch replied. I just need a change of vehicles so I can be incognito. I am riding too heavy to have the law on my heels!"

"Fuck the police!" Drako said with added emphasis. "I just need something fast to slide on these suckas in later on."

"Well this bitch got that 5.0 Hemi in it, so it should suit your needs." Enoch told him.

"You damn right it will! Them suckas will never see me coming, being that you already got the limo tint on this muthafucka!" Drako was amped up.

"You already got a tag for that muthafucka?" Enoch asked him.

"Quit playing! You already know that we keep stacks of the Kansas temps. It's 29 days left on the one on there, with the V.I.N. numbers from a clean ride. Just come holla at me if you need a new one." Drako feeling that he had answered all Enoch's questions satisfactorily, just sat there smoking, waiting to see what Enoch would decide to do.

Enoch counted out the money and gave it to Drako, grabbed the trash bag containing his money and dope. He removed about 2 grams from the brick and also gave it to Drako. He put both of his newfound Barettas in his waistline, grabbed his Carbine-15, cellphones, then hopped out the Challenger. Drako followed suit, tossed Enoch the keys to the Mustang, and thanked him for the lookout. The other homies saw that it was Enoch and gave him their greetings as well as their admiration for the heat he was carrying.

"Aye bro! If you are trying to get rid of that burner let me get it so I can put it to some good use." Enoch just gave Drako the thumbs up, before he hit the door locks on the keypad, and hopped in the Mustang. He started the car and admired the roar of the engine, put it in gear, and got right back into traffic. Handling the cars performance had him at Keisha's house in no time flat.

He loved how the car handled, and was disappointed that the ride was over so fast. He called her to let her know he was in the parking lot headed inside. He hopped out the car, trying to hide the Carbine-15 under his shirt. This wasn't the type of area where anything went unnoticed, and Enoch wasn't looking for unwanted attention. Sis was at the door when he approached, she was looking like she had a fight with yesterday and yesterday had won.

As soon as Enoch crossed the threshold, and the door was closed, Keisha tore into him.

"Where the fuck is my cousin, and what the fuck you got going on that is so important that your ass was willing to wake me up from my sleep Enoch?" Enoch not used to being talked to in such a way quickly responded.

"One it's damn near noon! Two Karter is good. Just finishing up the job."

"Finishing up the job?" Keisha asked. What the fuck you got my cousin into now?" Enoch just kept walking towards the kitchen without bothering to answer Keisha's last question. Once there he dropped his bag containing the money along with the brick on the table, pulled out a chair, and sat down.

"Aye you got some smoke?" Enoch asked her.

"Nah I don't, but I do know who got that cookie." She responded, while never taking her eyes away from his goodie bag.

"Call whoever it is and order up a couple of zips." Enoch said while placing guns on the table.

"Boy you doing too much! Put them guns upstairs in Kelly's room!"

"I gotcha Sis." Enoch said, just as Jay, Keisha's man, walked into the room, scratching his balls. Enoch got up from the table, picked up his guns and goodie bag and went upstairs to do as Keisha asked. He walked into Kelly's bedroom expecting to find it empty only to be surprised by the sight of seeing Kelly laying in the bed sleep.

What really got his attention was the fact that she was laying there in nothing but her thong panties. Enoch just stood there in shock, admiring the view for a full two minutes. After breaking the trance, he put the Carbine-15 and one of the Berettas on the shelf in the closet. He put the other Beretta in his waistband at the small of his back, took another glance at Kelly, then proceeded to return back downstairs with his goodie bag in his hands. As he entered the kitchen he overheard Keisha and Jay whispering, which they stopped as soon as they noticed his presence.

"I got all the answers you are looking for. Please just stop that whispering cause it makes me paranoid." Enoch said to no one in particular while returning to his seat at the table.

"Boy ain't nobody whispering!" said Keisha.

"Okay whatever." Responded Enoch. "Did you call your peeps about the smoke?"

"Yeah it's on the way. He said it's $400 a zip for that cookie." Keisha informed him.

"Cool." Enoch said while counting out the money. He gave Keisha $1000.

"That's enough for two zips and a couple of extra dollars cause I need you to make a run to the grocery store. I need two large Pyrex measuring cups and the largest box of baking soda you can find. Make sure you add some things you need around here to your purchase so you don't look suspicious." Enoch instructed her.

Keisha just stood there counting the money as she listened to Enoch's instructions. When she was done she gave the $800 to Jay to pay for the smoke, then turned her attention back towards Enoch.

"You still haven't told me shit about what's going on or where the fuck my cousin is!" Enoch gave her a look that said be cool before responding.

"She's fine. Sis I promise to tell you everything when you get back."

"Okay nigga you better!" Keisha shot back with a twist of her lips, before leaving to go get herself together.

Jay came and sat at the table across from Enoch, who was now tearing the packaging off of the brick. Enoch looked up at Jay for a second before returning to his task.

"You fuck around with this shit my nigga?" Enoch asked Jay who declined with a shake of his head.

"Is where all this shit came from going to show go knocking on my door?" Jay asked him.

"Nah my nigga. I promise that you have nothing to worry about." said Enoch.

Jay was a thorough ass nigga himself. He felt he had to ask so he could be prepared for whatever was to come. Keisha walked back into the kitchen and informed them that she was about to head out. She walked over and gave Jay a kiss.

"You want anything while I am out baby?" she asked him.

"Nah I am good, just make sure you get some juice and some fruit snacks." Jay told her.

"Aye yaw got a scale up in this bitch?" Enoch asked no one in particular, which both of them responded in the negative.

Enoch dug in his pockets and gave Keisha another $200 and told her to go purchase one from the pawn shop on Independence Ave. She took the money, said her farewells, and left out the door. Enoch took a $100 bill, rolled it into straw, and snorted a line of coke up both nostrils. The drug took its desired effect immediately. Enoch just sat there, cleaned his nose, stretched out his legs, and leaned back in the chair.

He picked up one of the phones off the table and dialed Randy's number. He wanted to ensure him that everything was good and that their meeting for later on that night was a go. He also wanted to be sure he was smart enough not to put anybody else in the mix. Bodies had dropped and he couldn't trust everybody to keep their mouths closed if or when the heat came down. The phone rang on the other end five times before it was finally answered...

Chapter 12

*J*oker sat at his desk in his study, infuriated about his home being violated like that. For the life of him he couldn't think of anyone who had the balls to disrespect him in such a way. He was pissed at Danny and Rico for their slip up, which in turn set the ball rolling for today's events to transpire. If they weren't already dead he would kill them himself. He sat there caressing the butt of the Calico sitting on his desk, wishing he had a target to empty all 100 shots into.

Focusing on the screen of his IPad, he was sure that this would be taken care of very soon. Movement in his peripheral vision caused him to look up at the monitor on the wall. "About fucking time!" he said to himself. He got up from his seat and headed to the door to greet his visitors. As soon as he opened the door he tore into the group of men. "What the fuck took you muthafuckas so long? I should be in this shit alone cause you lazy muthafuckas aren't worth the money I am paying you!"

He turned his back on them and went back to his study without waiting for a response. None of them were going to give him one anyway. One look at the gun and the ugly red welt on his face, and all 4 henchmen knew that saying nothing was best. After shutting the door behind them they followed Joker to the study. When they entered the study, Joker was sitting at his desk staring at them, as if they were the ones who had violated his home. The leader of the group Javier, was first to break the silence.

"Boss where's Danny and Rico? I don't see their truck outside."

"They are downstairs in the game room. Go get them for me." was Joker's reply, not willing to pass up the opportunity to show how he got his name.

Javier gave a nod to one of the other three henchmen, who promptly got a move on. Joker just sat there in his chair with a smirk on his disfigured face. Javier and the other two henchmen stood there bewildered, not understanding what was funny. As far as they knew, what they were here for wasn't a laughing matter. It didn't take long to find out what the joke was, when the henchman returned from downstairs visibly shook.

"Well?" Javier asked him. "Where are they?"

"They are both downstairs dead." said the henchman.

Joker just sat there, still smirking. "It usually happens that way when you take your job too lightly!" said Joker.

"Boss I don't mean to question your judgment. Why would you kill them here?" asked Javier.

"I didn't you stupid puto! They allowed themselves to be caught slipping by one man. I wanted you to see what it looks like when you lose in this business. Now that we have that out of the way we can now get to the reason in which you are here. The person responsible for your brothers downstairs used them to gain entry into my home. He also did this to my face, raped my woman, and took things that didn't belong to him. The rat bastard also took the cheese! Which is how you are going to find him and make him wish that he never fucked with LA Emme!"

"Gotcha boss. How are we supposed to find a man who we have never laid eyes on, in a city we are only slightly familiar with?" asked Javier. Joker took his hand away from the gun and slid the IPad across the desk to Javier.

"It shouldn't be too hard to follow the dot." said Joker. "This should lead you right to him. Javier picked up the IPad still puzzled. "What you are looking at is a GPS tracking App, linked to a tracking device hidden in the stacks of money I had stored in the safe. Seems like having it there was a better safety measure than having those two dumbasses following me around pretending to protect me."

Javier was starting to take the insults personal. No matter what they had done they had paid for their slip up with their lives, and they were also his brothers. In his mind Joker was taking the insults a little too far not to be La Emme.

Joker could tell that his insults had hit a soft spot, which was his intentions. He wanted to arouse their anger, which would in turn heighten their ferocity. "Get those two out of my basement and go track down the puto responsible. The money and drugs you find are yours."

Javier didn't need to hear anything more. He was willing to put the work in for free, the money was just an added bonus. He instructed the other three henchmen to go get the van and load their fallen brothers inside. After all three of them had left the room Javier stayed and asked the last few questions that he had for Joker.

"How much money am I expecting to find?"

"More than enough" Joker replied. Javier wasn't so sure that any amount of money could be worth the lives of his two brothers.

"What else are we looking for when we catch up to this man?" Javier asked him.

"About 12 kilos and 9 pounds of ice. Oh yeah he has my jewelry as well. Not that I really care about it, but it should be easily identifiable to you. The beacon on this locator isn't moving, and its been just over an hour since he left here. Hopefully you'll catch him with his pants down as he almost literally caught me."

"Boss you never told me how he got in here. I know you have this place well secured as most banks." said Javier.

"A story for another time, which is something we don't have to waste at the moment. Right now you have a job to do, and I have a woman to attend to. It's best that we not leave our duties waiting."

With that being said Joker stood up, picked the gun up off the desk, and walked with Javier downstairs to the garage. Danny and Rico had already been loaded up and the crew was in the van waiting on their leader. Javier with nothing else to say, hopped into the front passenger seat. Joker hit the button opening the garage for them, and watched them pull off into the day.

He stood there for a moment, hoping that they got the job done without leaving as much of a mess as had been made in his garage. He closed the garage and headed for the bar. He was going to have a drink while he now waited for the cleanup crew to arrive. He thought about the woman he had upstairs in his tub. How would she respond when she realized what had happened to her here? He questioned his thoughts, hoping it was true when they said sharing dramatic events brought people closer together.

Chapter 13

*K*arter woke up from what she felt had to have been a short nap. She was certain that it couldn't have been too long, due to the fact that the water she was sitting in was still lukewarm. Her head was clear and the only thing in her mind was making it out of this house in one piece. Right now apparently her and Joker were still good, but she wasn't sure how long this would remain to be true. She noticed that there was a giant bath towel sitting on the stand next to the tub.

She assumed it was left there for her because it wasn't there when she had first got in the water. She stepped out of the tub and dried herself off. She didn't see her clothes, so she wrapped herself in the towel, proceeded down the hall, in search of Joker. As she was making her way down the hallway she heard voices coming from inside a room she had yet had the chance to investigate. One of the voices belonged to Joker this she was sure of, but the other she was not familiar with.

She could only hear bits and pieces of what was being said, so she put her back flat against the wall so she could eavesdrop. She was also hearing voices and other three racket coming from down towards the garage area. After focusing on what was being said in the room Joker was in she could better hear what was being said.

"How much money am I expecting to find?" the unknown voice said.

"More than enough." she heard Joker reply.

"What else are we looking for when we catch up to this man?" the unknown voice kept asking questions.

"About 12 kilos and 9 pounds of Ice. Oh yeah, he has my jewelry as well! Not that I really care about it, but it should easily identifiable to you. The beacon on this locator isn't moving, and it's been just over an hour since he left here. Hopefully you'll catch him with his pants down as he almost literally caught me." Joker was starting to let his irritation show in his voice.

When Karter heard this, she damn near lost her breath. Enoch had left her here to fend for herself, as well as had fucked her in the ass. However, she was convinced he had done so to protect her. She had to find a way to warn him before he was killed by whoever it was that Joker was sending after him. She would be damned if she went through all this for nothing. Her love for Enoch made her automatically look for a way to protect him.

She heard them wrap up their conversation, so she creeped her way back to the bathroom as quietly as possible. She did a quick look around to see if any of her clothes or her watch were sitting anywhere around. Nothing! As she was finishing up her search of the bathroom she heard heavy footsteps making their way towards the direction of the bathroom, so she quickly snatched off the towel and sat on the toilet.

Just as her ass was getting settled on the seat Joker was crossing the threshold. Surprised by seeing her sitting there he stopped in his tracks.

"Hey, didn't mean to intrude. Just came to make sure you hadn't drowned." He had a smile on his face as he said this, which made Karter feel better about her position.

"Nah, I am okay. It's just that my ass really hurts." said Karter.

"I'm so sorry about that baby. Is there anything I can do? Anything that you need?" he asked her.

"No other than give me some type of clothes to put on, since I am sure my pants are destroyed." replied Karter.

"Can do." was all Joker said before he walked off. In what seemed like seconds to Karter, he was back with one of his oversized button up shirts. "I have to make some calls so I can get this placed cleaned up, and some other things that are needed he told her. "When you are done in here the bed is yours. Rest easy for a while and I got you as soon as I have this business handled." Joker told her.

"Thank you." was all Karter said before reminding him that she was also still hungry.

"I gotcha babe." he replied before leaving her to her business and returning to his study.

Karter heard him make his way down the hall so she got off the toilet and put on the shirt, which fit like an oversized onesie. Once dressed she made her way to the bedroom. Upon entering she noticed her clothes in a heap on the floor. She saw her watch on the dresser and wondered should she try to contact Enoch with the walkie.

She picked up the watch and laid in the bed, contemplating her next move. After a couple of minutes she tried to reach him getting no response. She tried again getting the same result. She sat the watch down on the bedside nightstand, and laid back on the plush pillows. The long night had finally won out over her adrenaline, so she allowed sleep to take her...

Chapter 14

*J*avier watched his brothers being placed in the incinerator with nothing on his mind but the task at hand. He glanced at the Ipad in his hand making sure the beacon didn't move. He wanted revenge as well as the added bonus of the drugs and money he was sure to be where the beacon would lead them. He wouldn't drop a tear because this was part of the life they all signed up for. The reason he was in in this warehouse on the West Bottoms was because they were always prepared for what could happen if they slipped.

Rico and Danny weren't the first to fall victim to the wrong side of the violence of the game. This wasn't the first Viking funeral he had attended and if he continued to live this life he was sure it wouldn't be his last. He watched as his other three brothers just stood there looking at the fire as if their brothers would rise again like Lazarus. Javier had seen enough. There was work to be put in and he was ready to get to it.

"Hey carnals gear up! It's time." Each one of his brothers started gearing up getting ready to go put that work in. Kevlar vests, MP-5 submachine guns, face masks, and Glock 19's is what each of them were suited up with. They all four hopped back into the black van headed to their destination. Javier told them that when they got to where they were going to be patient and wait on his signal.

"No matter what you see don't allow your emotions to make you jump the gun." They were crossing the 12th St. Bridge. They took Highway 35 South heading in the direction the beacon leads them. The further south they got the more Javier could tell this highway was taking them off course. He could see they needed to go east so they exited onto 435 East coming close to their destination.

The locator indicated that they needed to travel further south so they exited Highway 435 South onto Highway 71. At this point Javier could see that they were very close so he informed the rest of the hit squad to be on high alert. Riding dirty like this in this van with his brothers' blood still visible on the floor, him and his crew knew they couldn't even risk getting pulled over by the law. They were all hardened killers who wouldn't hesitate to put that work in on the pigs given the chance.

After about ten minutes of driving south on 71 the beacon became very red and started flashing so Javier told the driver to take the next exit. They got off at the top of a hill that didn't have much traffic, the locator said go right so that's what they did. Just as it was designed to do, it led them right to Belton Inn Motel. Javier was excited about this because he knew this would be easier than if they were lead to a house in a residential area. They pulled into the parking lot canvassing the area trying to get a feel of the layout...

****

The man behind the check in desk of the Belton Inn watched the van pull up the drive happy to see patrons coming to check in. Business could be better at this time of year and every dollar was needed. He watched the van ride past the check in building and swore he didn't remember anyone checking in driving such a vehicle. He watched the flat screen monitor on the wall, tracking the van by camera to see which room they were going to.

As the van drove past one camera that was close enough to see inside the van he could have sworn he saw the driver was wearing a full face mask with all black on. He wasn't sure but now his interest was now piqued. He continued to watch the van circle back and noticed the passengers face was covered also along with all black clothing. He was no detective but he knew trouble when he saw it. He continues to watch the van as it went to the other side of the parking lot and park. He saw the panel door open, and didn't wait for the first boot to hit the ground before he picked up the phone and called the law...

****

After circling the hotel parking lot, Javier was certain he found the room he was looking for. He had told his crew to be on alert but they were so focused on the task at hand they only had eyes for what they came for. As soon as Javier gave the okay the driver backed into the parking spot right in front of the room in which they were lead. In ten seconds flat Javier and two of the henchmen were out the van and kicking the door in like the task force guns drawn, ready. They ran in not knowing what to expect but not caring. When they got in the room they noticed it was empty.

Javier instructed one of the henchmen to go check the bathroom and under the bed; while he stood with his back to the door they had just forced in, his gun was still in position to fire. Both did what they were told quickly shaking their heads indicating the negative. He told them to tear the room up hoping they would find at least half of what they came for. After about five minutes of tossing the room up, one of the henchmen came out of the bathroom with two duffel bags. Javier checked the bags to be sure of their contents, after nodding the affirmative to his two brothers they turned to leave the room and head back to the van.

As soon as they hit the threshold they heard automatic gun fire. Javier and his brothers jumped back into the room to take cover not sure where the shots were coming from. Alligator crawling to the window he lifted himself up enough to look out the window attempting to see what was going down outside. From the sound of the shots, now he could tell the automatic gunfire had to be coming from Smoke the driver, the MP-5 had a distinctive sound he was familiar with. What he wasn't sure of was who was now returning the fire. Now looking out the window to his dismay he saw multiple police cars in the parking lot with officers using their cars for cover now firing in the vans direction. Smoke was firing at them over the hood of the van giving them more than they could handle.

Javier relayed to his brothers what he saw out there and informed them that they had to make their move now or be sitting ducks. Javier believed that the element of surprise would be the best way to go. No way was he willing to be trapped in this room waiting for backup to come and seal their fate. Using hand signals, he simulated a countdown for when they would make their exit. As soon as he was down to a balled fist all three hopped up and stepped out into the parking lot opening fire on the police totally catching them by surprise.

The fully automatic gunfire was more than the Belton Police were prepared for. Instantly they took cover as their cars were peppered with bullets. All three made their way to the sliding door continuing to fire as they did so. As soon as they got the door open, Smoke stopped firing and hopped in the driver's seat. Bullets hit the side of the van as Javier hopped in with his two brothers who were both trailing him. They were both hindered by the fact that they were each carrying one of the duffle bags while firing at the officers at the same time.

Mondo was the first one of the two in the van, bag and all. Ghost wasn't so lucky, just as he was getting ready to make his way two shots hit him directly in the head spraying blood and brain matter onto the side of the van as well as the back of Mondo. Smokes foot was already pressed on the gas unaware that one of his brothers had fallen victim to one of the policeman's gunfire. The van bounced as he rolled over his brother unknowingly as he was trying to get them out there.

Now that they had both hands free Javier and Mondo were giving the police hell with MP-5s in one hand Glock-m19s in the other. As they were riding past the police cars they had them in the open without cover and gunned all six of them down. They continued to head to the exit at a high rate of speed. "Fuck, Fuck, Fuck,!" Javier screamed at the top of his lungs hitting the ceiling of the van at the same time. "We lost Ghost back there!" he informed Smoke.

Smoke never said a word as he was focused on driving. He got onto the highway heading towards the inner city. He had the van doing over a hundred miles an hour hoping to see no more police. Javier told him they needed to ditch the van and find new wheels fast. Smoke nodded in the affirmative dipping in and out of traffic. He got off on the next exit which was Red Bridge, he made a left heading straight towards the 7-11 half a block up the street.

They pulled into the parking lot at a high rate of speed. Finally having luck on their side there was a woman at the pump filling the tank of her brand new Honda Accord. Smoke slammed on the brakes and they all hopped out, glocks in their hands in case anybody wanted to make trouble. Smoke hopped in the lady's driver's seat relieved to see the keys already in the ignition, Javier hopped in the front passenger, while Mondo hopped in the back toting the duffel bag they got away with.

The lady just looked at them like they had lost their minds, but didn't utter one word as they put her car in gear and tore out the parking lot snapping the gas nozzle off spewing gas everywhere. Mondo bent some blocks, made his way back to the highway heading back towards the warehouse. None of them said a word as they were forced to silently mourn another one of their brothers all in one day...

Belton Police cars infested the Belton Inn parking lot. Officers were eyeballing each other with this knowing look. Six of their own had been gunned down in cold blood and they wanted the culprits, dead if they had their way. Shell casings littered the parking lot along with the body of one the perpetrators. Detectives O"Malley and Springer had been assigned the case so they had instructed officers to tape off the scene and mark the location of all the shell casings that were found.

They had already been to the front desk and interviewed the hotel manager. They had obtained a copy of the license that was used when the room they were now standing in front of was rented. They had already faxed it to the station so the photo could be run through NCIC. They had first run the name through in their car, but the name didn't match the photo. While waiting to hear back from the station they decided to canvass the crime scene. They had officers going door to door checking to see if they could find eye witnesses, not that they needed them because they had pretty much everything on tape.

Detective O'Malley kneeled down next to the body that was laid out in the parking lot and pulled the sheet back that now covered the body. He wanted to pull the mask off that covered the perps face but couldn't due to the fact that he had been shot in the head twice and he didn't want to destroy any evidence. He pulled the shirt as well as the Kevlar vest the perp was wearing up and noticed that everywhere there was skin there were tattoos from the waist up. He held the MP-5 that was found next to the body in a plastic bag as well as a Glock-19 that was found in another.

What interested the two detectives the most was the duffel bag full of cash. They couldn't understand what happened here today especially since this large amount of cash was left behind by the culprits. Two men in dark suits approached them while they were doing their investigating, with looks on their faces like they meant business. "Who's in charge here?" the tallest of the two asked.

He was 6'4, with a slender build and dark as a chocolate bar. His partner was Caucasian, shorter standing about 6'0 feet even, with the physique of a bodybuilder. He just stood next to his partner never saying a word like a sentinel. "Who's asking?" replied O'Malley from his position kneeled next to the body. He never even bothered looking up at who he was taking to do the fact that he was studying the tattoos and was sure this would be his last chance due to how official the voice sounded.

"I am Special Agent Jones and this is now my crime scene." he said. "Before you decide to show any resentment to my authority, I want you to know that I understand this is your jurisdiction and also that the fallen officers may have been close friends of yours." He continues. "I am only here to make sure the proper amount of attention is paid to what happened here today and that whoever is responsible is brought to justice and prosecuted to the fullest extent of the law. As a sign of good faith I offer you this."

Special Agent Jones handed O'Malley a computer printout. "It's the real name of the man who rented this room, it took our computers five minutes to match the face on the bogus I.D. with the real name." O'Malley accepted the paper as he got to his feet, still never uttering a word. Special Agent Jones continued his spill. "His Name is "Enoch Jackson and he spent some time inside for armed robbery and gun possession. No known address or next of kin." He went on to explain. "I am sure finding him will be like finding a needle in a haystack being that he absconded from parole two years ago."

O'Malley just stood there staring at the picture for a few more seconds before handing it to Detective Springer. O'Malley finally making eye contact with Special Agent Jones asked, "Why tell me all this since you are clearly here to take over?". Jones replied.

"Take over no, take the lead yes". "I figure since you and your boys are probably emotionally fired up by what's happened here that you'll work harder to catch who's responsible". O'Malley just stood there staring in Jones' eyes as he talked nodding his head in confirmation, as if he understood exactly what Special Agent Jones was saying.

Jones finished by saying. "You and your partner finish up gathering your Intel here, inform your officers about what's going on and who we are looking for. Be sure to tell them our lead is just a person of interest, me and my partner here will be at our communications vehicle over there as soon as we inform those news teams about what's going on here."
He said looking towards the news crews that were in the crowd behind the yellow tape. They departed with handshakes and went on to their designated tasks……..

Chapter 15

*J*ay was sitting in front of the television watching his stories. Everyday him and Keisha would smoke and watch soap operas. He had left Enoch in the kitchen sitting at the table zoned out. Jay knew firsthand what cocaine did to a person. He had been raised in the crack era and watched both of his parents taken from productive members of society to crack heads overnight. By the age of 12 he was left in a position where he had to fend for himself.

His father had been sent to prison for robbery and his mother turned into a streetwalker. She got a welfare check on the first, gave him $100 out of it, and this is what he was forced to survive on for the month. Sometimes his mother would not even give him that due to the fact that she owed her whole check out before she got it. Jay did go to school as much as possible so he had a slight understanding for economics. He started taking the money he got from his mother and flipping it.

He would buy a couple of ounces of weed from his uncle Mike break it down, roll it up into blunts and sell them for $5 a pop at school and to friends in the neighborhood. One day they brought a drug dog through the school unannounced. They found Jays stash in his book bag during gym class. He was expelled for possession of marijuana for the rest of the school year. Jay found himself stuck in the projects all day with nothing to do. He took his hustler mentality and started slangin rocks right out of his mother's apartment.

Once she found out she became one of his biggest supporters. She would have people over at all times of the day or night getting high copping from Jay. Needless to say, ever since then, Jay never received $100 a month from his mother again; and he never returned to school either. Now a full grown mature adult, there he was sitting on the couch waiting on Keisha to come back with the tools he needed to ply his trade. He had been down on his luck as of late but Enoch had informed him that all that would change for the better.

Enoch walked into the room with the bag of money in his hand. He was kinda off balance as he walked in front of Jays view of the television. He said something about needing to go use the bathroom which Jay just nodded his approval. As Jay sat there watching his stories his program was interrupted with a newsflash...

"This is Harper Smith from Channel 5 News and I am here on the scene where 6 Belton Police Officers were gunned down in a vicious gun battle here in the parking lot of the Belton Inn. There are reports that there were at least 4 culprits one of which was killed here on the seen also. The suspects were seen leaving here at a high rate of speed heading north in a Black late model Chevy Econoline Van. Hold on reports just in that 3 men in all black just abandoned a black Econoline matching the description given earlier in our reporting and carjacked a woman for her car at the 7-11 off of Red Bridge before making their escape. We will continue to give you coverage as we learn more about what's happened here. There are detectives as well as Federal Agents here on the scene who will be giving us reports on the details here shortly. Until then we will return you to your regularly scheduled program...

Jay could give a fuck about some officers being killed, shit as far as he was concerned he was happy somebody was evening the score. He was brought out of these thoughts by a knock at the door. He went to answer it happy to see it was the weed man. He let him in, gave him his money right at the door, got the weed and let him right back out. This was a little different than how they usually dealt, but with the kitchen table covered in coke and Enoch walking around here carrying a small trash bag of money he was not about to take chances on his business being anybody else's. Jay went and sat right back in front of the television, rolled him a backwood, and laid back to relax and finish watching his stories...

Enoch made his way to the top of the stairs one step at a time. The coke he was ingesting was starting to get the best of him. That and the fact he hadn't had a full night's sleep. In order to get to the bathroom, he had to go through one of the bedrooms. He decided to use the entrance in Kelly's room hoping to get another eye full of that banging body she was rocking. He entered the bedroom and to his delight she was still laying there on her stomach, ass swallowing the string of the thong she was wearing.

He put the bag of money down on the bed right next to her pillow as he made his way to the bathroom. He left the door open as he undid his Rock Revival Jeans, pulled his 8 Inch dick out and relieved himself. He shook himself off, left his pants undone and made his way to the sink to wash his hands and put water on his face.

Out his peripheral vision he could have sworn he saw Kelly watching him. He shook his head and told himself it was the drugs and that he was tripping. He heard movement coming from the bed. He turned the water off, grabbed a paper towel off the roll on the basin top, and made his way back to the bedroom.

As soon as he re-entered the bedroom he was struck with a sight that made him get an instant hard on. Kelly had shifted positions to laying on her back with her legs open. One leg was drawn up so her foot was flat on the surface of the bed, the other drawn up also, but this one laid so the outside of her leg was also flat against the mattress.

Her arms were stretched out above her head, ample breasts on full display. Enoch felt he knew she wasn't sleep and also knew what she was up to. Being that he knew it wouldn't be long before Keisha returned he immediately tried his hand. He walked over to the side of the bed and instead of retrieving the bag of money he licked his fingers, reached out and tweaked Kelly's nipples.

Kelly responded by letting out a soft moan while biting her lower lip. This was all the encouragement Enoch needed. He went over to the door and shut it, came back to the bed and kicked his shoes off. He climbed up on the bed and placed his head between Kelly's legs. He moved her panties to the side and stuck his tongue right in her pussy. She instantly changed positions to lying flat on her back, legs spread wide open.

Enoch was now fucking her with his tongue while applying pressure to her clit with his thumb. He alternated the pressure by rotating his thumb in a circular motion. After about two minutes of this Kelly reached down and grabbed his head attempting to shove his whole face in her pussy while gyrating her hips. Enoch was all in now, he took his left hand and pulled her panties all the way to the side so he could have an unobstructed view of the pussy.

He dove in face first taking Kelly's clit in his mouth while sucking and twirling his tongue on it as fast as he could. She started bucking her hips, riding his face like a mechanical bull. "Oh shit, Oh shit OOOhhh"! was all you heard constantly being repeated over and over by Kelly. All of a sudden her body started shaking and convulsing making Enoch aware of the fact that she was coming all in his mouth. He just kept sucking while he had both arms locked around her legs so she couldn't scoot away.

After she stopped shaking he climbed up between her legs and slid his dick into her now soaking wet pussy. She expelled a breath, put both hands behind Enoch's head, and pulled his face to hers sucking her juices off of his tongue. Enoch was to hilt up in Kelly's pussy, stroking her deep and fast as he could. He was now definitely enjoying himself, he had been wanting to fuck Kelly since forever, he wanted to really put it down but knew he had to finish and get out of here before Keisha returned.

He took Kelly's right leg and placed it over his shoulder. He picked up his intensity as he stroked the right wall of Kelly's, pussy going in deep as possible. "Oooh Boy Give Me That Dick"! Kelly said a little too loudly for Enoch's liking. He felt the pressure building up in his dick and knew he was about to cum. He kept stroking Kelly's pussy, pulling out at the last second and nutting on her leg. He got up from the bed and went in the bathroom to wash up.

When he came back into the room Kelly was still laying there flat on her back chest rising and falling like she had just ran a marathon. Enoch opened the bag of money, grabbed one of the $5000 stacks out and laid it next to Kelly's pillow. He then leaned over her gave her a deep tongue kiss. After breaking the connection, he put his pointer finger up to his lips signaling Kelly to keep it quiet. He then put his shoes back on, checked his appearance, and returned back downstairs with his bag of money feeling like today had to be his lucky day...

Chapter 16

Karter woke up with Joker standing over her just staring at her. His look made her uncomfortable cause she didn't know what was on his mind. She felt something wet and sticky on the inside of her thighs and immediately started to wonder what had he done to her who while she was sleeping. He pointed to a spot on the bed causing her to look at what he may be pointing at. Karter's eyes bucked showing how shocked she was to be laying there in a blood spot that apparently came from her.

She was sure she wasn't bleeding when she went to sleep, so now it was no longer a question she was sure Joker had done something. Had he found evidence that she was responsible for what happened here earlier? He eased her worries when he asked her was she okay, and did he need to call an ambulance. After her fears were assuaged she noticed a sharp pain coming from inside her rectum she hadn't paid attention to before now. She put her hand between her legs and noticed that this is where the blood had come from.

Apparently her getting right in the water and soaking after the brutality Enoch had put her ass through had kept her from bleeding and noticing how bad she was damaged. Karter was embarrassed but knew this was how she would make her exit. She got up and ran to the bathroom noticing that she had also soaked through the shirt Joker had gave her to wear. She hopped right in the shower washing the blood off her also giving her time to think of what to do next.

She washed herself thoroughly wincing as the soap burned the tear in her ass. She got out of the shower to an awaiting Joker standing there with a towel and a brand new Victoria's Secrets Pink sweat suit. Karter took the towel to dry off just looking at the clothes, her eyes filled with wonderment.

"The clean-up crew has been here and gone as well as my sister Maria who stopped and picked up the clothes for me. I felt it was the least I could do since it's my fault yours got destroyed." Joker said answering her unasked question.

"Thank You." Was all Karter could muster while trying to get herself together.

"She also brought you some lotions, underwear, and other female toiletries." Joker told her while eyeing the goods sitting next to the tub in a gift basket.

"Do you think you need medical attention?" He asked her. "I also have a doctor on call who can come out if needed."

"I think something is ripped inside of me and I really appreciate your offer but I would like it more if you just took me to the hospital." "Or is this something else that you would have someone do for you?" Karter asked showing a little attitude. Joker just looked at her like she had just slapped him.

He really liked Karter but had just come to the realization that he didn't really know this woman or what to expect from her. He had never been in a position where he actually cared before so he didn't really know how to show it. He expelled a breath of defeat realizing that eventually he was going to have to allow her to leave and before he had the chance to make up for what he had allowed to happen on his watch.

"Okay you just finish getting yourself together here and I'll take you to whatever hospital or doctor's office you want to go to." Joker told her before turning around and walking out the bathroom.

Karter did just as he told her to, she dried off, put on lotion from the gift bag as well as body spray. She liked the underwear his sister had picked out but dared not put them on before taking about a quarter roll of toilet paper and making a makeshift pad so she wouldn't bleed through her clothes again. She also looked for some type of Vaseline or petroleum jelly to help soothe the tear. After getting dressed and doing what she could to fix her hair she went to find Joker. She found him in his study on the phone.

As soon as she stepped into the room he took the phone from his ear and told her give him one minute and he would be ready. Karter went to the bedroom got her watch off the nightstand and put it on. She slipped into her shoes, and stripped the bed while she waited on Joker. He came into the room saw what she had done and told her it wasn't necessary but it was appreciated.

He took the covers from her arms and carried them downstairs to the washroom on the way to the garage. He hit the door locks on the Phantom and told Karter to get in the backseat and lay down so she could be comfortable. She did as she was asked although she was sure this request had more to do with her not knowing where this house was as much as it was for her comfort. Joker closed the door for her, hopped in the driver's seat and after hitting the garage door opener he hit the road.

After about three minutes of driving Joker asked Karter where she would like to go in which Karter replied Research Medical Center. He just nodded his head in compliance. After about another five minutes Joker broke the silence.

"Karter whatever you do please do not tell the doctors there exactly what happened to you. I would rather you told them we were experimenting with an anal sex toy or whatever else you can come up with please just don't tell them what really happened!" Joker pleaded with her.

"You don't have to worry about me doing that, I am not stupid." She said.

"I don't mean to seem callous, it's just that last night's events won't stop there, and I don't want the police connecting dots back to me or any of my affiliates." With that being said Joker just drove while Karter rode laying in the backseat....

Chapter 17

*K*eisha came in the door just as Enoch was making his ascension to the bottom of the stairs. She was carrying a couple of bags and instructed Jay to get up and go get the rest of them from the car. Jay who was smoking his blunt just looked at her like he didn't wish to be bothered before getting up and doing as she asked. Enoch stopped on the second to last step so she would have room to get the bags in the door, this leaving his groin area elevated to the same height as Keisha's head.

She turned to look at him wrinkled, her nose like she smelled something, gave Enoch a, "No you didn't look," shook her head and made her way to the kitchen. Whatever Keisha may have been thinking she wasn't about to let it fuck with her getting this money.

Her and Jay hadn't been having the best of luck lately, so Enoch and what he was bringing to the table was right on time. Jay had fucked off their savings, re-up, as well as what she was bringing in doing hair. He had all of a sudden thought he could beat the casinos cause he watched tournaments on ESPN.

What a fool he had made of them both, him for trying her for allowing him to.

Keisha knew one thing; he wasn't putting his hands on the paper this time. She placed the bags on the counter as Enoch came and sat at the table, instantly taking his makeshift straw and snorting another line of the coke.

Keisha looked at him and asked, "Did you come down here to snort all that shit up your nose or to get money?" with an attitude.

Enoch laid his head back allowing the drain to flow to his brain. He just looked at Keisha while pointing at the table, "This is nothing compared to what's in store for us!" Enoch told her with an air of arrogance.

Keisha didn't say a word as she started putting up the groceries. She was placing a big box of baking soda on the table in front of Enoch when Jay came into the kitchen carrying the rest of the groceries, as well as a bag from Jay's Pawnshop. He placed the bags in the middle of the kitchen floor causing Keisha to look at him like he was crazy. He carried the pawnshop bag to the table and sat down giving Keisha a look like you know what's up. He opened the bag took the scale out and placed it on the table.

All of a sudden he hopped up from his seat and ran towards the front room, when Keisha and Enoch heard the television being turned up they just looked at each other and started laughing. Jay walked back into the room wondering what was so funny. Keisha already knowing what he was thinking by his look said, "Boy you a mess, can't miss a minute of those stories." while still laughing. Jay just sat at the table and rolled him another backwood.

He gave Enoch his zip he had purchased for him and gave the rest of his to Keisha. Jay wanted to get his smoking out the way now cause he wasn't about to chance cross contamination while he was fucking with the coke. As soon as they were done blowing they all got straight to work. Jay was grinding up two and a quarter at a time in the Pyrex with a hot sauce bottle. He was planning to cook this shit into crack using both Pyrex's at the same time.

Keisha already had the pots on the stove boiling. Enoch was separating the coke and weighing it up in eighths. Once things were operating smoothly Keisha Broke the silence by asking Enoch where was her cousin. He expelled a breath, stopped what he was doing and just laid back in the chair he was sitting in. He just started his spill no longer able to keep the truth from them.

"Karter is the reason we are here with what we have now. We got put onto a lick that was sure to change all our lives forever. I got her put on at this strip joint."

"STRIP JOINT"!!! Keisha screamed interrupting him.

"Not what you think just let me finish." Enoch told her.

Keisha wasn't so sure due to all the bullshit he had involved her cousin in the past, but she shut up and allowed him to continue.

"As I was saying I got her put on with my man hoping to hook this fish and it worked a little better than planned." Enoch said while looking at Keisha like I know what you are thinking. "I planned to use her as an accomplice to gain entry into his house, accept I improvised and gained entry another way."

He continues on, "Shit got a little filthy, and in order to make sure my baby wasn't implicated I was forced to leave her with the mark. She is good I am sure of it. But that's all I can tell you without killing you." Enoch said before rolling himself a backwood of his own. He didn't care about coke getting on his shit because he did it all.

Keisha asked, "So what's up with Karter?"

"I am sure she will be contacting you shortly. She has no way to reach me. I was forced to get rid of my watch and phone." answered Enoch.

Jay just stood there at their stove whipping up the work while this exchange was going on. His attention was on the task at hand as well as the television. Only story he wanted to hear was All My Children. His stories as well as the one Enoch was telling was interrupted by another news bulletin.

"This is Harper Jones from channel 5 news reporting to you from the scene of the Belton Inn Parking Lot where six officers and one suspect was gunned down in a gun battle where detectives are saying over 150 shots were fired. We have been informed that we do have the name of a person of interest the Special Agent in charge would like to talk to. We now turn over the broadcast to Special Agent Jones."

"I first want to give my condolences to the families of all the fallen officers. I want to ensure you that we will be doing everything in our power to make sure all culprits responsible will be brought to justice and prosecuted to the fullest extent of the law. Right now we don't have much to go on, other than there was a large amount of cash found at the scene seemingly in the possession of one of the perpetrators who is now deceased. We also have the name of the man who rented the rooms apparently connected to what happened here today." He stated.

The person of interest is six feet two, two hundred and twenty pounds with a muscular build. Here is a picture we have on file. We ask that if you come into contact with this man to not approach him being that he may be armed and dangerous. Contact your local law enforcement or call Tips Hotline (816) 555-5633 and notify us to his whereabouts and allow us to handle things appropriately. Again he is only a person of interest, we are in no way implying that he was involved although he does have an open warrant for parole violation." The detective ended with.

"Okay. There you have it his name is Enoch Jackson; he is a black male six feet two with a muscular build. Here is the picture again. That is all we have for now just tune in at five for more updates, now back to our scheduled program"... By this time Enoch and Keisha were standing in front of the television. Enoch was in a daze not believing what he was hearing and seeing. He was sure he hadn't been followed. He had used a fake I.D. to get the rooms yet they knew exactly who he was.

He heard them say there was a large amount of cash found at the scene but nothing about drugs which kinda eased his worries. Keisha was just staring at him burning a hole in the side of his face. "Enoch are you sure that Karter is okay?" Keisha asked him breaking the silence between the two. Kelly came down the steps dressed in a Gap jogging suit with air maxes to match. Before Enoch could even answer Keisha's question she asked why did they have the T.V. turned up so loud while turning it down.

Enoch just looked at Keisha and nodded giving the only answer he was willing to give at the time. They all returned to the kitchen with Kelly scrunching her face up. "What the fuck you in here cooking got the whole house smelling like that Jay?" She saw the glass Pyrex's as well as the weighed up portions of coke divided up on the table and had her answer. "Okay I see yaw in here doing big things!" Kelly said to no one in particular. She sashayed her ass straight to the refrigerator opened it and took the juice out so she could pour herself a glass.

"Enoch do you think you could give me a ride to the mall?" Kelly asked. All three of them just looked at her like she had lost her damn mind. Keisha was wondering what she was planning to do at the mall being that she had just last night asked her to borrow $20 and also because she hadn't come up with her portion of the rent. Keisha didn't like how she was looking at Enoch when she asked for the ride but didn't let on that she was bothered by it. "Nah sis can't do it; got things I have to handle." Enoch told her.

She never asked Keisha for a ride which heightened her curiosity even more. She would be sure to ask Jay how long Enoch had been upstairs while she was gone, she wouldn't put anything past her fast ass little sister. Jay had finished with the first 41\2 and dumped both Pyrex's on some paper towels on the table to dry. Like the professional he was he was filling both Pyrex's with coke and baking soda ready to get right back to the task at hand.

He doubled the portions since he now knew how the coke came back. Enoch now sat at the table rolling another blunt. The newscast didn't really phase him as much as the knowledge that most of last night's work had now went down the drain. His mind was in survival mode trying to figure out what would now be his best move. After finishing rolling the blunt he fired it up picked up one of the phones off the table and dialed a number...

Chapter 18

*J*avier and his crew had made it to the warehouse safely and also gotten rid of the Honda Accord they had carjacked while making their escape. They now all stood around the table sorting the drugs that they had retrieved from the hotel room. Mondo was in a somber mood because Ghost was his real brother.

Yeah "LA Emme" made them all brothers but it was different when it was blood. He broke the silence by expressing his displeasure with how today's events had unfolded. One moment they had a stranglehold on the underworld wreaking havoc and killing anything that tried to get in their way to all of a sudden have three brothers taken out the game in one day.

"So what's next? Do we call in reinforcements?" Mondo asked. Javier just pondered on his question for a moment before answering. He wasn't sure himself because he was sure the brothers back in California wouldn't take the news well. He also knew that calling for reinforcements could open a door that he wouldn't know what was behind it. Reinforcements might also come with someone else taking the lead. He had to show he could handle things here so he knew it would have to be them three that would have to put in the work.

"Nah we gotta handle this ourselves." Javier told Mondo. "After we get this here sorted and put away I have to call Joker to give him the news and see what other information he may have for us. The bag of money we left at the scene had the tracking device in it, and I have to be certain it can't be tracked back to Joker or us in any way."

Smoke who was the hothead added his thoughts, "I don't give a fuck about Jokers fat ass the pinche puta! Him slipping was the cause of all this, you yourself Javier said he never revealed how the pinche miata had gotten into that fortress his lives in anyway. For all we know he set us up using us as scapegoats to take the fall! If a muthafucka violated the sanctity of my home where I lay my head I would have insisted on personally putting the work in myself. He sits his fat ass in the house with some bitch none of us has ever heard of or even saw talking about its his girl! If you ask me, we call home and get the green light on his ass!"

"Nobody asked you!" Javier screamed at the top of his lungs. Javier had a real problem with anybody bucking his authority. If his crew started thinking they could think for themselves then they may think they no longer needed him. In Javier's mind Smoke was right, but he could never let on to that. Javier knew that Joker held up to 500 kilos, 2500 pounds, as well as hundreds of pounds of methamphetamines built into a trap in the wall of the safe house.

Taking that would leave them rich, but also with death on their heads as well as everyone in their families. You didn't fuck with the cartels shit and live on this planet safely. Killing Joker would be useless without taking the stash so it was best to just see what he knew and go from there.

"Okay you two finish up with this here and get it put up. I will go call Joker and arrange a meeting. He needs to tell us all he knows about who we are now dedicated to finding as well as who this bitch is he is so caught up on." With that said Javier left them to the task at hand and walked off to call Joker.

****

Joker answered the phone on the third ring, "What's up?"

"Things didn't go as planned." was all that was said on the other end.

"Can any of you follow the simplest directions? I practically gift wrapped the black bastard for you!" Javier was seething on the other end, being talked to like an underling by Joker was not on the list of things he felt he would ever go for. He kept quiet while he tried to calm himself causing Joker to keep running his mouth. "Maybe I need to make a call to see if I can get some real competent help sent out here."

Now too angry to hold back Javier reiterated, "As I said we need to talk! You haven't told us how this man gained entry into your house, who he is, what he looks like, or who this girlfriend is you have all of a sudden! I am sure who you plan to call back home wouldn't like to hear how they have invested countless millions establishing a CLOWN that was so easily infiltrated! Your subtle threats fall on deaf ears, but they are open to hearing anything that would help clear this mess up."

Joker just sat at his desk pondering over what he just heard Javier say, being honest with himself shit didn't sound right the way Javier put it. He wasn't "LA Emme", they wouldn't like to hear about their brothers dying out here because of him slipping. He quickly changed his tone and asked Javier when would he make his way out to the house to clear the air. Javier told him it would be about an hour and hung up on him. Javier sat there after the phone call totally satisfied with himself.

He had taken the position of power from Joker with a couple threats of his own and would make sure it stayed this way from now on. Listening to Smoke had prepared him for this conversation but he would never tell him know that, control was his drug and he didn't like to share it. With a smile on his face he returned to his brothers to make sure they had finished stashing the drugs so they could prepare for their meeting with Joker's fat ass...

Chapter 19

Jay had been at the stove for hours non-stop. The work would all be cooked and ready when he finished with this last batch. Keisha and Enoch were at the table weighing and packaging the dope preparing it for the takeover they had all agreed on. Jays chef skills was bringing back an extra ounce off of every eighth. That means a brick would have come back to 52 zips had Enoch not have kept 2 1/4 in powder for himself. All in all, they should have about 50 zips when Jay was finished.

Keisha had already had one of the neighborhood smokers that lived in the apartment next door test it out and he left with his eyes bucked promising that it was the best dope he had smoked in years. Kelley had called one of her friends for a ride to the mall and had been gone for a while. Keisha still felt something was going on between her and Enoch due to the fact that Kelly kept unnecessarily bumping and brushing against him multiple times.

She didn't let on that she was concerned because she wanted to be sure she wasn't tripping. As they were packing the dope up for sales Enoch broke the monotony, "Check this out, I want 600 a zip and the rest belongs to you two. 4 zips belong to you and Jay. Sis off the top for the lookout. I really appreciate yaw coming through for me. All in all, I should be receiving a little over 27 thousand from you two. Is that cool?"

Both Jay and Keisha were nodding their heads in agreement at the same time. Selling the shit wholesale, they knew they could make at least a thousand dollars a zip being that the town was kinda starving for good dope.

Enoch continued with what he had to say, "I know you both heard the news reports so you know that once I leave I won't be coming back here. I can't afford to bring heat to this crib at all! I have some shit I need to handle so I can kill this heat and clear my name. Karter will be calling here fa sho. It shouldn't be long now so Keisha make sure you answer your phone from any number. Just in case you are wondering I didn't have anything to do with happened at that hotel, but I did rent the rooms where it seems like things went down. I don't know how or why things went down but apparently I wasn't as careful as I thought. Keisha I need a bag to carry this money in."

Keisha left the kitchen and came back with a Louis Vuitton backpack. Enoch took the bag and put 10 of the 5000 dollar knots inside of it. He gave the rest of the money to Keisha and informed her that it belonged to Karter. He felt that by giving the money to Keisha that it would be safe and also that they would believe him when he said she was okay. Regardless of what they thought Karter was his woman and if she didn't show up soon he was going to get her even if he had to go knock on Jokers door.

Enoch picked up his cellphones, his weed, as well as his coke and put them in the backpack also. By this time Jay was dumping both Pyrex's on paper towels on the table. Enoch grabbed his weed shoved it in his pocket along with a couple of packs of the backwoods that Keisha bought earlier. He walked over gave Jay a pound Keisha a half hug and headed out. He went upstairs to Kelly's room grabbed his heaters placing both Baretta's in his waistband and the Carbine 15 in his bag.

When he got to the mustang he pulled the phones out his bag plugged them into the car chargers, took two toots of the powder, rolled himself a blunt and was in traffic. He called Randy's number and waited for him to answer. "What's good?" was all Randy said when he answered the phone. "I am out and about heading towards the meetup spot." Enoch said in response.

"Yeah okay, I am at the movies right now and can get there in like forty minutes" "Cool" was all Enoch said before hanging up. Just thinking about meeting Randy at Gates Barbeque had Enoch's stomach growling. He had been doing nothing but getting high all day while over Keisha's, and here it was like 8:00 P.M. and he had yet to eat anything. He rode east on 12th St. headed towards 435 south. Enoch planned to take the out the way route, not wanting to chance riding through the inner city...

Chapter 20

*K*arter had no clue which direction he turned or was headed when they pulled away from the house. She didn't even bother trying to sit up and look because it was much more comfortable to just lay back there due to her injury. She was also focused on what reason she would give the medical staff at the hospital. Before she knew it she was awaken by Joker's voice telling her that they had arrived. Karter didn't even know she had fallen asleep back there, let alone made it to the hospital already.

She sat up in the back seat and got herself together. Her ass was still hurting. She couldn't help but to think of Enoch and wonder what the fuck he was doing. Where was he at? They made their way into the hospital and she explained to the triage nurse what her ailment was. She stuck with the sex toy story. She was rolled back immediately to her room once she signed her consent forms and received a wrist band. She knew Joker wasn't going to leave her side so she was glad when they asked him to step out while they administered an examination.

She took that opportunity to tell her nurse that she didn't want him to return to the room. She made up some story about him being possessive and overbearing. She informed the nurse that she wanted to get away from him and would be using other transportation home. She made sure to specify to the nurse not to call the police because that would raise his suspicion. The nurse expressed her understanding and said she would inform him she needed to be taken for an MRI. She then commenced to complete the task at hand. Karter requested a phone to use as she didn't see one in the room already.

The nurse returned quickly with a phone to plug into the outlet. Karter immediately dialed Sis number. She was the first person she called because she knew she had the best chance of reaching her and she could remember her number by heart. She answered the phone on the first ring. Karter had never been so relieved hear her voice in all her life. She gave her a brief story of what had taken place and that she needed a ride asap. Sis told her she was on the way. Karter was sure to tell her where to pick her up from, nowhere on the hospital premises that's for sure.

****

As soon as the door closed behind Enoch Keisha went to the door to make sure that it was locked then right back to the kitchen. She didn't waste a moment with her interrogation of Jay.

"So what was Enoch doing coming from upstairs when I came in the door earlier?" Jay just shrugged his shoulders wondering where was Keisha going with her inquiries.

"Boy don't just shrug your shoulders at me! How long was he upstairs?" Jay responded verbally this time. "He was in the kitchen stuffing his face with this bullshit before I left him there to watch my stories. He came out wobbling and told me he needed to the use the bathroom. He couldn't have been up there more than ten to fifteen minutes.

"Why?"

"Are you trying to tell me you didn't notice anything going on between him and Kelly?" Keisha asked him.

"Him and Kelly? The man was working non-stop like I was from the moment you came back. Now your flirtatious ass little sister; who knows what she was doing. Long time ago you tell me not to pay any attention to her now you expect me to be her investigator? I am glad I wasn't paying attention to her cause it would be me you would be accusing right now instead of Enoch! What I don't understand is if you noticed something why you didn't check it right then and there?" Jay said clearly agitated.

"Jay when I walked in the door I could have swore I smelled sex all on Enoch. He was standing there on the steps with his junk right at the level of my nose when I walked in." Keisha said.

"Once again" Jay asked "With you being the woman of this household why didn't you check that shit to make sure your suspicions were not just suspicions? All you had to do is go upstairs and follow your nose like Tucan Sam!" He was now laughing at Keisha while he puffed on his blunt.

Keisha's phone started going off. She turned from Jay and grabbed it out of her purse that was hanging on the back of one the chairs at the table. It was a number on the screen she was unfamiliar with but she swiped to answer anyway.

"Keisha where are you I need you!" Karter said hysterically.

"Karter is this you?" Keisha asked.

"Yes this is me and I need you to come and pick me up right now."

"Girl where are you? Your man just left here and told me you would be calling. He left your things here before leaving saying he had things to take care of." Keisha wanted to say more but knew better than to talk so openly on the phone.

"He's okay? Karter asked barely able to control her emotions.

"Yes he's okay but I have a feeling that he's in some deep shit. Where are you Karter?" Keisha asked her.

"I am at Research Medical Center. I need to get away from here fast so I need you to meet me at CVS on the corner of 63rd and Prospect." Karter told her.

"I am on my way; it won't take me any more than 10 to 15 minutes."

"Thank you Sis, I don't know what I would do without you." Karter said barely able to hold back her tears.

****

Karter buzzed for the nurse. She told her she needed to be discharged asap and asked the best way to get to the medical buildings from there, aside from the main ER entrance. The nurse explained how to get there and told her she would let the doctor know she was ready to be discharged. Karter knew that shit would take forever as it always did. If they didn't go back and get Joker soon he would be asking what the fuck was going on. At the same time, she knew she needed to give Sis enough time to make it to her from down north.

Karter got dressed, grabbed her stuff and headed on the journey to the medical buildings. She arranged for Sis to meet her at the CVS on 63rd and Prospect. She would camp out there until she arrived. She got to the medical buildings and made her dash from there. The further she got away from the building, the more nervous she became. She was glad that it was only a tear in her canal and would heal fine with ointment and no other penetration.

She got a little pissed thinking about that; she felt like Enoch had taken it too far. Then she began to wonder why Keisha made that statement to her about Enoch? She felt naked as hell. She kept looking over her shoulder and around the parking lot. Every headlight she saw had her spooked. She made fast strides as she headed to the store. She couldn't get to the store fast enough.

As soon as she made it to CVS she asked them for a phone. The clerk at the front explained they don't have a phone she could use and the closest pay phone was at the gas station across the street. Karter didn't want to walk over there and risk missing Sis nor possibly running into Joker who she wasn't sure or not was looking for her. But she wanted to call her and see how far she was. She decided to wait a few more minutes, hoping to see Keisha pulling into the lot.

Chapter 21

Drako, Tre, and his cousin Dink were strapped nasty, riding three deep, headed to where the sucka's were known to hang out. They were all high out of their minds off of the coke Enoch have given Drako earlier. They were riding down Prospect in the Dodge Challenger they had gotten earlier from Enoch. They had enough guns and ammo riding with them to fight a small war.

Drako was carrying a Glock 40 with a 30 round clip as well as an A.K. with a 75 round drum. Tre was carrying a AR 15 with a 90 rounder on it as well as what he called his bitch which was a 9mm Sig Sauer. Dink had two Mac 11 Cobray's that he had paid to have the firing pins altered on so that the guns were fully automatic. If Tre could have his bitch riding with them then it was only fair that Dink brought along what he called his baby mommas. "Cuzz I know that ain't one of those sucka's behind us is it." Drako asked. Dink who was riding in the backseat was sitting sideways with both guns in hand said "Make a few turns and if they follow us I am going to tear they ass up."

Tre wasn't with that plan he was a real killer so his advice was, "A Drako just hit those sucka's block so we can hit they ass up before they burn out. You know them nigga is hard to catch up with as it is. Nisha said them niggas looked like they were getting ready to head out when she called us. If that's one of them back there in that car behind us let them follow us so we can hit'em all up at the same damn time man." Drako made the next right turn, then made the next right turn onto Wabash headed back north. He noticed a couple sets of headlights coming behind him too fast for comfort. Tre let his window down and sat on the door balancing both guns on the roof of the Challenger waiting.

The headlights had made both turns with them and were gaining on them fast. Just as Tre was pulling both triggers on his Mac 11's they were slammed into by a car coming down the hill. The front passenger side of the vehicle slightly rose up off the ground causing Tre to start firing into the air while he fell off the window into the street. All of a sudden there were flashing lights everywhere and shots being fired at them from all directions. Tre tried to get up off the ground and return fire only to be gunned down by the officers in the unmarked cars. The

Challenger had stalled due to the collision and was taking fire from the officers as it sat there in the street.

Drako was ducked down under the dashboard with the A.K. in his hand waiting for his chance to get off shots of his own. He reached up above his head to turn the key over in the ignition to see if the car would start. As if God was with him his prayers were answered and the Challenger started right up. The shooting had stopped for a moment giving him his chance. He rose up firing shots out the passenger window at the car that had blindsided them. Two Officers dropped instantly.

He turned his attention towards the cars that were trailing him letting off shots out his rear window attempting to empty out the whole 75 round drum. Once he was satisfied that he could get out of there he dropped the gun on the passenger seat, put the challenger in reverse and dislodged himself from the car that had crashed into him. He then put the car in drive and shot off down Wabash doing 80mph. He shot through 39th street. without even stopping and made a left on 38th street.

He went straight another couple of blocks and stopped right before he got to Brooklyn Ave. He slammed on the brakes while turning the wheel to the left blocking off the whole street, he shifted the car into park and opened his door and hopped out. "Let's go Dink!! Let's go Dink!!! When his commands went unanswered he looked into the backseat only to see Dink laid out in the back with the top part of his skull missing and blood all over the backseat, his eyes staring at nothing in particular, his mouth slack.

Drako reached into the back seat and grabbed the AR-15, made sure he had his phone and took off running through the backyards. After making it to 35th street. he came out of the backyards and took off running across the bridge. Trying to make it as far from the scene as possible he crossed the bridge and kept running until he made it to Highland. He ran into the backyard of the corner house and hid under the back porch. He took out his cellphone and called the number Enoch had called him from earlier...

Chapter 22

Karter saw Keisha pull into the parking lot and instantly felt relief. The cool summer nights' air was starting to chill her bones and she kept having this feeling that every car that pulled into the lot was searching for her. She didn't know why she was so shook, from what she knew Joker never even suspected her. Any sane woman in her right mind would want to get far away from a man who would put them through last night's events on the first day they had met.

Karter just didn't feel right due to the fact that Joker really tried to protect her when his life was also in jeopardy. Thinking about it she wasn't sure Enoch would have done the same for her. Thinking of Enoch, she wondered where he was and if he was okay. As she was getting in the front seat of the car with Keisha she winced as soon as the seat came into contact with

134

her ass. Keisha noticed her discomfort as well as the band on her arm and gave Karter a hug as soon as she got settled into her seat. She then loosened her embrace and looked at Karter deep into her eyes.

"Are you okay Karter?" she asked with as much concern as humanly possible. Karter just nodded her head yes while trying to hold back her tears. She was so relieved that she had made it through the night's events still alive and in one piece her emotions almost overwhelmed her. She didn't allow any tears to drop cause she didn't want Keisha to worry or start judging her for her lifestyle choices.

Keisha, always the big sister, could never miss her chance to play out her role. Since Karter never said anything Keisha just started talking as she pulled out into the night's traffic. "You know your man has been at my house all day since early this morning. He called me waking me up out of my sleep telling me to make sure my house was cleaned out because he was coming over with a life changing opportunity. You know Jay had fucked up all our shit right?" Karter just nodded her head to affirm she was aware.

"Well waking up hearing that things could be changed in an instant I did all he asked of me. I've been in the kitchen with that nigga all day while he was getting high and bagging shit up. He left a bag of money for you and all the work to me and Jay." Keisha now had Karter's full attention as they rode down the highway, she was listening hoping Enoch had not divulged information about the role she had played in last night's events. As they were headed past the 39th St. exit they noticed the Ghetto Bird circling in the air and a lot of police cars canvassing the area right off the highway.

Keisha didn't really pay it any mind as she kept driving and talking. "Yeah he set us back on our feet real nice like. The fucked up part about it all is there was a shooting involving police somewhere out south and they put Enoch's face and name on the screen as a person of interest." Hearing this Karter's eyes bucked and her mouth went slack. Keisha looked at her and kept talking to ease her fears.

"At the time the shooting went down Enoch was definitely at the house so I am sure he wasn't involved, but the Special Agent on the news still put an all-points bulletin out for him."

"Where is he now?" asked Karter.

"I am not sure, he left and said he had some business he needed to handle. I do have a number for him in my phone though. I don't know why I didn't say so already so you could have called him and told him you were okay. He was sure you were going to be calling me so I expect he would have wanted me to have you call him when you got the chance."

With that being said, Keisha dug into her purse, pulled out her cellphone, and handed it to Karter with it already dialing Enoch's number.

Enoch answered immediately, "What's up?" Karter just sat there saying nothing, filled with emotions that threatened to overwhelm her. "Hello?" Enoch said again waiting for a response.

"Hi," was all Karter could get out without her self-control failing her.

"Baby is this you?" Enoch knew how to turn on the charm at times which was a direct contrast to how he could be at other times.

"Yes this is me." Karter responded barely managing to keep her composure.

"Baby I hope you are okay. I have some shit to do to make sure we are covered then I will be straight to Sis's to get you. Are you sure you are okay?" he asked her again.

"My ass hurts boy!" Karter told him laughing in the process.

Enoch chuckled too knowing he was definitely going to hear it for that stunt he pulled. Still laughing at what Karter said he told her he was sorry and that he loved her and reiterated that he would be to Keisha's as soon as he got the chance.

"Please be careful and I love you too." Karter told Enoch before ending the call.

She handed the phone back to Keisha before letting her seat back some and closing her eyes. The day's events had taken their toll on Karter and she could now finally relax knowing her and Enoch had got away safe and sound. Keisha just looked over at her little cousin and said a silent prayer for them both. The life they lived with their men kept them on edge and sometimes in danger. Keisha loved her some Jay and wouldn't trade what they had or had been through for anything in the world. She just hoped God would continue to protect them as she navigated her way through the streets of Killa City on her way home.

She pulled into her parking lot located in the back of the apartments. She nudged Karter to get her up so they could go in. She dug into her purse and retrieved her compact Glock-40 and put it into her jacket pocket. In the projects you couldn't be sure what would happen or when so it was best to be prepared. Her and Karter walked in the door to find Jay sitting in his favorite spot on the couch smoking a backwood. As soon as he saw who had come in with Keisha he offered her the blunt and asked her was she good. Karter declined the smoke and told him she was good. She went right upstairs to Kelly's room and laid down on her stomach. She fell asleep just like that waiting on Enoch to call or come and get her...

Chapter 23

*E*noch was sitting at the pump at the BP gas station on 47th and Paseo. He didn't need any gas just somewhere to think and wait for Randy to pull up to Gates across the street. While waiting his phone rang which threw him off because nobody should really be calling these numbers. He answered on the second ring only to be surprised by Drako breathing hard and kinda hysterical.

"Cuzz I need you bad Cuzz!"

"Hey youngsta what I tell you about calling me that." Enoch responded.

"Cuzz I need you bad and now. I think the pigs just tried to off us! They jumped down on us and let loose on us, no warning or nothing!" Drako continued.

"What?" Enoch asked not really understanding what he was hearing.

"I am in somebody's backyard on the corner of 38th and Highland. I need you to come get me out of this jam before somebody calls the police on me Cuzz!" Drako told him breathing hard the whole time, barely able to get his words out. Enoch instantly put the Mustang in gear and tore out of the gas station heading up Paseo.

"Just stay on the line and say no more!" Enoch told him. "I should be there in three or four minutes be ready to come out when I say."

"Thanks Big Bro!" was all Drako could say to that.

"Oh so now that I am coming to save your bad ass I am big bro now?" Enoch said laughing attempting to calm Drako down. Enoch made the right turn off of Paseo onto 39th street.

"Come on out while the coast is clear." Enoch told Drako while sitting on the side of the street not knowing exactly which way he would be coming from. He didn't have to wait long, in less than 20 seconds Drako and his inherited AR-15 along with his Glock-40 were sitting in the passenger seat of the Mustang. Enoch got right on the gas and made some blocks getting the fuck away from that neighborhood. He handed Drako the blunt he was smoking hoping it would be enough to calm his nerves.

Drako was visibly shook and sweating heavy. After finishing the blunt Drako let the window down and threw out the dubee, he had tears in his eyes as he started talking. "Big Homie I don't know what the fuck just happened, one moment we was riding down Prospect trying to get to the sucka's block I spoke on earlier. We had got word that they were out there gift wrapped for us on their block. We saw a car behind us we thought it was them following us so we made some blocks trying to shake it and see if it really was on us." Drako didn't even seem to be taking a breath while he gave Enoch the whole story.

"We were heading down Wabash with the car still on our bumpers so we were getting ready to let loose on whoever it was. As soon as we hit the corner of 41st and Wabash a car slammed into us knocking Tre off the car into the street. Before I could react we was getting dumped on from all directions. I saw hella flashing lights which is how I know it was the pigs, cause they never announced themselves. When the shooting let up I raised up and let loose with the A.K. on them. I saw a couple of them drop but I ain't sure if that was cause they were hit or ducking for cover. I let the whole drum go and got the fuck out of there driving like a madman. Once I was far away from the scene with no one on my tail I blocked the street off and got ready to bail. My mans was laid out in the backseat with the top of his head missing." Drako continued.

"Cuzz I ain't never saw no shit like that before and wish I hadn't. That was my nigga I saw in that position with eyes staring at nothing, just empty. I took his bitch and got the fuck up out of there!'" Drako finished saying while stroking the AR-15 from barrel tip to stock.

"So you telling me yaw were ambushed by officers in unmarked cars?" Enoch asked Drako.

"Homie that's exactly what I am saying!! I never heard of the pigs reacting like that to what they may perceive to be a stolen car. Being that the car was hot you know they will be looking for the driver so they can put them bodies on me. I ain't got nothing but these two bangers and the money you gave me earlier. I need bread so I can shake the city for a while." Drako responded.

What Drako had just told him had Enoch's mind racing. He knew he had probably been the reason for Drakos downfall, the car he had traded him hadn't been mentioned in the news bulletin but that didn't mean they hadn't identified it as the vehicle he was driving when he rented the room. He felt responsible so he had to keep it 100 and help Drako get the fuck outta dodge. Looking at Drako stroking his gun with his burner gloves on gave Enoch an idea…

Chapter 24

Joker was pissed. The nurse at the hospital kept giving him the run around on where Karter was and if she was okay. The nurse even tried to get him to have his face looked at to which he declined. Now that he couldn't find the girl he was getting nervous. While waiting in the waiting area he saw one of the news bulletins about the shooting at the Belton Inn. Police officer's dead were always bad for business especially if you were involved in any kind of way. From experience he knew they would leave no stone unturned trying to get to the bottom of what happened.

He saw the face as well as the name of the person of interest and made sure to keep it logged into his memory. If this was also who he was looking for he had better hope the police caught up to him before he or his henchmen did. He knew now that this ordeal at the Hotel was what Javier was referring to. He felt exposed sitting there at this hospital not knowing where this girl was or what she had told them. The nurse couldn't even be convinced to tell him what name she had been admitted under.

Javier and the crew would have a field day with this one and he had no explanation for it. Joker came up with the idea that it would be best to lie about the girlfriend he told the crew he had. He felt it would be best to keep them off balance with what he knew about what he saw on the news. He could also meet them at neutral spot using the heat as an excuse. He really didn't want to get into the conversation about the girl, he still wasn't sure and needed time to figure it all out.

He left the hospital without a second thought as to where the girl was or if she was okay. He hopped into his car and started it up but never put it in gear. He pulled out his cell phone and dialed Javier's number hoping he didn't answer. His luck wasn't so good today because he answered on the first ring.

"Almost to the house now!" was all Javier said.

"Change of plans, I have to come to you!" Joker said in response.

"Why?" Javier asked.

"Cause my friends made the news and I can't risk the heat coming to the house." Javier knew exactly what Joker was referring to and couldn't argue the fact that Joker was right. It pissed him off that the position of power he had acquired over Joker may be short lived. He had to have his story straight before they met up or Joker just might have to call for the reinforcements due to the fact that Javier and the crew may have to get low.

He told Joker to come to the warehouse and hung up the phone. He didn't know what Joker knew being that he hadn't heard anything but he was almost sure him or any of the crew hadn't slipped up at all. He informed Mondo and Smoke about what was up and told them to be prepared for anything. He still really wasn't trusting Joker right now and wanted to be sure that the crew was aware of this fact.

Right now he had no other choice but to play along and see how things went; but if Joker tried anything that would be his ass for sure. With these thoughts on his mind, he pulled the dark blue Cadillac Escalade into the parking lot hit the button for automated loading dock doors and pulled the S.U.V into the port. He hopped out the truck after parking it and immediately went to arm himself and instructed Mondo and Smoke to do the same.

He told them why the change of events as well as who they were expecting. He was stern while giving his directions to Smoke to be prepared for anything and to not open his mouth at all. He explained that it was best to not do any talking and to allow Joker the floor. He wanted them to understand that he wasn't 100% sure about him and felt that allowing him to control the conversation would give him the chance to talk himself into a corner. He gave the green light for Smoke to deliver the kill shot if they felt threatened or if Joker wasn't willing to give them the information needed for them to navigate their way out of this ordeal.

As Javier was giving his instructions he saw Joker pull into the lot on the monitor on the wall that all their security cameras were feeding into. He told Mondo to go open the doors so Joker could pull his car in. He put the finishing touches on what he felt he needed to say to Smoke.

"We are in a fucked up position little brother. We lost some of our own as well as the bag of cash that would have instantly gave us more freedom of choice. We don't even know who we are looking for or who may be looking for us. We need answers more than anything right now and I need you to keep a cool head so we can get them. I have gotten us this far; all the way from the wretched streets of Zacatecas. Trust me and I promise to get us further than we imagined with more than we ever dreamed."

Smoke just nodded his understanding and never said another word. He was taking his post in his favorite spot in the corner of the makeshift office in his recliner chair. As soon as his ass hit the cushions Joker walked in with Mondo trailing right behind him. With no introductions needed Joker walked over and took a seat behind the desk while Javier and Mondo took their stations; one standing at the entrance the other standing right in front of the desk.

Joker took a moment to look each one of them in the eye before he started talking. "Last night's events are the beginning of what has us in this predicament. I take full responsibility because I believe I am at fault. After leaving the strip club last night I allowed myself to slip up due to my love of the trade. I fuck with strippers because I feel I have the ability to see behind the mask a woman wears by how she dances. I can tell if she is controlled by the money or by her needs. Women unlike men have the ability to do the worst jobs in the world with a smile and you would never know the work is killing her. It comes from their paternalistic instincts that are ingrained into their DNA. I identify with their plight so I support their cause, you can call this my way of giving back."

He continued on, "Last night I saw something I had never seen before which was a woman who had no earthly business being on stage. She was uncertain of herself and her dance moves were awkward and unskilled. I admit it turned me on and drew me to her like a moth to a flame. When she finished her set I had Danny go to her dressing room and retrieve her for me. She came to the booth gave me a bullshit lap dance which confirmed my analysis. I struck up a real conversation with her and built something with her that seemed realer than usual. I allowed this to have me make the decision to take her with me with the intentions to save her from a life I didn't feel she was built or prepared for. Me, her, Danny and Rico all rode together to the house where Danny and Rico left us alone."

Joker kept on with his explanation, "Before you ask, yes I was careful. I searched her, took her phone and powered it off and made sure we weren't followed. Danny and Rico left in the Escalade and took her phone with them. We hit it off very well at the house. We conversed on real life topics as well as how we both ended up in the lives we were living. We made passionate love and had a good time. All the lovemaking made us hungry so I attempted to reach both Rico and Danny on their phones but neither was answering their phones."

"Danny was wasted due to the fact that it was his turn to really turn up as they call it. Rico was alert and on it going off my observations, but no matter what they both always stayed in good enough condition to answer the phone or handle any situation. After trying to reach them for at least ten minutes I turned on the monitor and noticed they were parked right outside in the driveway apparently sleeping and allowing me the courtesy of complete privacy. Like I said before I had broken protocol with my actions so they were apparently following my cue. I threw on some clothes and went outside to the truck to get in their shit for their foolishness and was surprised by the intruder who we are now searching for." Joker was telling it all.

"I admit he caught me off guard and unsuspecting. I had to have alerted him to my presence by trying to open the door to their truck. He got the drop on me and forced me back into the house by gunpoint. I don't know how he got the drop on our brothers, but he must be a professional willing to kill. He seemed to have known who and what I was as well as what he was looking for. My fear for my life as well as my fear for what could happen to the girl on my watch caused me to give him the proceeds from my last drop as well as the trick bag out of the safe. The fucker ass raped the girl right in front of me and branded my face like a steer! I have video footage of him, but he was masked up so that won't help much but due to what happened at the hotel I have a name." Joker said to them.

Just mentioning the hotel made all three sets of their eyes widen in interest. "Yes you guys made the news and the Feds are now on the case. They mentioned the name Enoch Jackson as a person of interest and flashed his picture. From the height, weight, and build descriptions we are all now looking for the same man. I will get in touch with some of our contacts to see if we can't get more info but this will have to wait until the morning. The girl who you may still be suspicious about I had to take to the hospital, she woke up in my bed in a puddle of her own blood. Her ass was damaged that bad so I had no other alternatives." Joker let them know.

"Where is she now?" asked Smoke. If looks could kill he would have died instantly from the look Javier threw at him. Joker seemed to not mind the question and didn't notice the silent exchange between the two so he answered with no hesitation. "As far as I know, still at the hospital. I don't believe she is an important piece to this puzzle but if she proves to be involved in any way or could be of any assistance she shouldn't be hard to find. I have footage of her on the security system and Randy who owns the club has to have contact information for her."

"So with all of what you have told us this leaves us where?" Mondo asked. "Well it leaves us with two options. Do we hit the streets hard in search of our prey or do we allow the law to do our jobs for us? I don't believe you three are willing to accept my opinion so that leaves the choice up to you. I just want you to know whatever your choice is, I will assist however I can." When Joker said this all three of the brothers just looked at each other communicating without words. It was in their pedigree to finish what they started so it was no question about what they wanted to do.

Javier turned back towards Joker and began talking, "Our blood has been spilled so this has become personal business! We need you to get us pictures of this fucker and for safe measures pictures of the girl. We also want access to any and all info you obtain on the matter as soon as it comes to you. We will handle this. Just know that when it's all over with you will owe us and you better not have a problem paying!" Joker just looked at Javier dead in eyes and nodded his head showing he agreed to the terms. Joker stood up from his chair and headed to the door to the office. Mondo just stood there without moving giving Joker a death stare.

Joker just stood there in front of him returning a stare of his own, "Oh I will have the package with all you should need ready by noon tomorrow but until then you should be able to find the picture of who we are looking for on any off our local news stations. They really want answers about those dead police officers! After Joker said this Mondo looked over at Javier who gave him a head signal to move out the way so Joker could exit. Mondo followed as Joker hopped back into his car. He raised the door so he could leave and didn't close it back until he saw him leave the parking lot and drive off down the block. He returned to the office to find Javier and Smoke tuned into the local news, they were now on the scene reporting on more officers down as well as another dead and one seriously wounded. All three just looked at each other and shook their heads.

Chapter 25

Special Agent Jones and his partner Special Agent Sloan were perusing over the evidence gathered from the Belton Inn shootings. They were inside the command center vehicle working at the island in the main room with some other agents. Oswald Jablowski AKA "Ozzy" was in charge of getting a count of the money that was in the duffle bag left at the scene by the perpetrators. He and his team were also in charge of trying to backtrack the tracking device found inside one of the bundles of money. He walked into the main room where Agent Jones and the other agents were huddled around the island with a report of his findings in hand.

As soon as he approached them Agent Jones diverted his attention from what he was doing and looked to Ozzy with a look of expectation.

"Well what have you come up with?" Ozzy didn't waste any time giving a report of his findings. "Well there was well over $300,000 in that bag along with this." In his hand he held the miniature tracking device he and his team had found inside one of the stacks of money.

"What's that?" Agent Jones asked."

"It's how whoever we are looking for found themselves here at this hotel to retrieve those two bags. Judging by what we got from the hotels video surveillance, the culprits came looking for this money as well as whatever was inside the other bag they got away with. I think Enoch Jackson somehow got his hands on something that didn't belong to him. Lucky for him he wasn't there when they arrived or there would most likely be no lead alive left to tell us what we don't know."

"I have Agent Ohashi attempting to reverse track the devices original position. Hopefully that will lead us to where the bags originally came from or at least where they were being tracked from. I bagged and tagged the money and have it ready to be sent to headquarters for possible fingerprints, as well as the bag it was retrieved from. I also have Ohashi and his team attempting to enhance the quality of the video from the surveillance tapes. Hopefully we can come up with something that may help in identifying the suspects if we ever need to."

"Good work Ozzy." Agent Jones told him. "I can't think of anything you may have missed accept giving me a timeframe on how long it may take to trace the signal from the device back to its original source."

Ozzy was happy Agents Jones caught this because it gave him a chance to show Agent Jones how him and his team were super-efficient and went the extra mile. He wasted no time giving Agent Jones the answers he was looking for.

"Well it would only take us minutes once we find which service provider was used with this technology, after that we find the nearest cell tower from where the signal originally pinged from. I think Ohashi has some other tricks up his sleeve that may even get us closer, expect some kind of results we can move on within 24 hours."

Agent Jones just nodded his head at the information, confirming that it was good work. He took the report from Ozzy's hand then told him to get back with him as soon as he had something new to report. Turning back to his team at the island he was right back to the business at hand.

"What do we have from the van Agent Sloan?" Agent Jones asked. "

"Well there were multiple shell casings found that match the ones found at the scene here. There were also trace amounts of blood found inside the van that have already been gathered and are on the way to the lab for analysis. Hopefully the DNA is already in our database, but if not it would help in identification when we find our suspects. Once forensics is finished with the van they will turn it over for fingerprinting. There are no VIN numbers on the dashboard and tags the although registered to the same make and model van don't belong to this one. We seem to be dealing with professionals if you ask me Jonsey." Agent Sloan responded.

Agent Jones didn't like being called by his nickname in front of his coworkers but he allowed Agent Sloan to get off without a reprimand.

"Who talked to the lady from the 7-11? I don't see a report on what she saw or if her car was equipped with OnStar, or if her cellphone may have been left in the car at the time. If there is even a chance to make it any easier on us I expect one of you to figure it out! I want that car! I want to know if there is any blood in it so we can know if one or all of the suspects have been hit by gunfire during the exchange with the officers. If there is a loose hair I want it! And I want that shit yesterday!" Agent Jones wasn't as impressed with his own team as he was with Ozzy's.

He didn't mind pushing people further than normal limits which is why he was in charge. Interrupting his tirade was another agent with reports of another shooting involving officers. When he heard that the car believing to be the car belonging to Enoch Jackson was involved he grabbed his jacket off the hook on the wall and hightailed it to his unmarked vehicle. Agent Sloan wasn't two seconds behind him and together they tore out of the parking lot into the night heading to the scene of the latest officer involved shooting. They were not alone, Two more unmarked cars and a news van followed not far behind...

****

Flashing lights from emergency vehicles and police cars, officers milling about securing the crime scene, bystanders from the neighborhood standing outside of the yellow tape attempting to get a closer look at the results of the carnage from the gunfight. Agent Jones pulled his unmarked car as close as he could to the scene before him and Agent Sloan hopped out looking for the officer in charge. After flashing his badge then being allowed entry into the taped off area they were escorted to Detective Roper the officer in charge of the crime scene.

"Detective Roper this is Special Agent Jones and Special Agent Sloan. They are here because they are heading the investigation into the officer shootings that took place at the Belton Inn and believe that this shooting here has a connection."

"Thank you Officer Gonzales, I got it from here I need you to ensure none of those people standing around break the perimeter. I also want you to get someone on top of finding witnesses and taking their statements. Agent Jones and Agent Sloan follow me."

Detective Roper lead the way to the heart of the crime scene. The bodies had already been removed but the cars as well as the firearms and shell casings still laid in the street where they had fallen. There was glass scattered everywhere from the crash as well as car windows being shot out. The Agents were focused on the multiple bloodstains on the pavement. When Detective Roper noticed what had their attention he gave them the rundown on what happened there at the scene.

"So far what we know is the officers involved we're working as a unit undercover in the neighborhood. At around 8:00 P.M. they came across a black Dodge Challenger fitting the description of the vehicle that was put on the all point bulletin earlier today. They followed the vehicle while calling in to see how they should engage. It's since then been reported by one of the officers involved, that the Challenger tried to make some evasive actions through this residential area." Det. Roper explained to them.

"One of the passengers in the vehicle came out the window armed and perched himself on the window of the passenger side of the vehicle pointing his weapons at the officers trailing them. Just as the suspect starting firing another unmarked vehicle crashed into the Challenger with the intentions of putting the car out of commission as well as throw off the aim of the suspect. Upon impact the suspect fell off his perch and into the street seriously injured, the cars were lodged together keeping the suspects from attempting to escape apprehension." He continued on.

"The officers from all three cars opened fire on the remaining suspects in the Challenger which I am not sure at this point was warranted. The suspects returned fire from what the shell casings appear to be an AK-47 assault rifle, they fired at least 50 to 100 shots, right now we aren't sure. We have three officers' dead on the scene and two more seriously injured. We have one of the suspects under police watch at the hospital who is also seriously injured, one more dead, and at least one who seems to have gotten away." Roper finished.

"Have you identified any of these suspects yet?" Agent Jones asked the detective.

"No, but that is exactly what we are working on at the moment. They had no identification on their person and the one that was injured is currently in surgery at Truman Medical Center." Roper replied.

"Where is the Challenger?" Asked Jones.

"About eight blocks away from here, one of the bodies was retrieved from the backseat alongside with a few firearms. The AK-47 assault rifle was one of them and it was still warm to the touch when officers retrieved it from their car. All weapons from the car have already been transferred to our forensics department downtown. We wanted to be sure on their ballistics and hope for fingerprints or DNA. Agents my officers are dead and their families have lost their sole providers. I am sure I don't have to explain how personal us at the KCPD will take this. I am not sure these officers followed protocol when they came in contact with the suspects' vehicle being that they were undercover, but that won't matter to my guys. They won't admit it but they will be out in full force looking for retribution for this mess we have here." Detective Roper wrapped his synopsis and just stood there looking at the Agents hoping they understood.

Agent Jones masked his true feelings about all he had just heard, put on his best business like smile, stuck his hand out so it could be shaken by the officer, and after doing so got right to business.

"Look Detective Roper I don't have enough time to explain how much of a mess this whole day has been for our city. We have nine dead officers as well as others injured. I have one lead and I am not sure if he is already in the morgue or still running these streets. I need you to get these men in your custody identified right now. I am sure you want to help me prevent any more blood from being shed."

He continued," I also need you to tell me exactly where I can find this Dodge Challenger so I can get my team to work on it. I want you to take this card and call me with a full report of your findings here. I think it's tied to my scene and if so that means this is my case also. You will be my man on the ground in charge here although I will leave a couple of my agents here to make sure all evidence is being properly handled as well as to make sure you have all the resources you need." With that being said Detective Roper told the Agents exactly where they could find the car, bid them farewell, and got back to work processing his crime scene.

Special Agents Jones and Sloan arrived on the scene just in time to see the Challenger being hooked up to the tow truck. The body had already been removed from the backseat as well as the guns that were found inside. Agent Sloan conferred with the Officer in charge of the scene and took command of the process. He had the Challenger towed to the FBI crime lab to be immediately processed. He wasn't taking any chances on allowing one piece of evidence to get mishandled. Officers had been killed for reasons he still wasn't sure of, but he had a hunch that it involved drugs and the money it produced.

When anybody lost their lives for these reasons he took it personal. Since losing his father to a drug overdose it had been his sole purpose to rid the world of drugs. Impossible a task as this was he still put his all into accomplishing this goal. As he watched the tow truck drive off down the street he was distracted by the lights of the camera crew from the news team. He never was convinced if whether their reporting helped or hurt a case.

For all he knew who he was looking for was getting updates about their investigations via the Channel 5 news. He snapped out of his thoughts, and told himself it didn't matter. Whoever was involved was going to pay for the carnage that had happened in this city over the past 24 hours. Right now all he could do is wait and allow his team to be the professionals that they were and be ready to go wherever the evidence lead them…

Chapter 26

"*H*ello welcome to Tomfooleries my name is Chad and I'll be taking your order today. May I interest you in one of our specials?"

"Nah no specials, but I will take a double shot of Patron and a glass of water." Enoch told the waiter.

"I'm cool on the specials also but you can bring me two doubles of Remy V.S.O.P. if you have it." was Randy's response.

"Yes we have Remy which is also one of my favorites. I'll have those drinks for you in a jiffy. Will there be anything else?", the waiter asked.

"Nah we good for now but we will be sure to tell you if that changes." Randy told the waiter.

When the waiter left the table Randy didn't waste a second getting down to the business of the meeting. "So how did things go?"

Enoch was skeptical about talking about the situation cause of how dirty it had gotten, but he was compelled to say something. "It went as planned without a hitch. I didn't come out with what we discussed was supposed to be there, but I can't complain. I have 40 racks in the car for you which leaves me and Karter only a little over a sixty to split.

Things got a little dicey, but it was nothing I didn't prepare for."

Randy just looked at Enoch trying to read him, to him 40,000 was cool but he knew Enoch was downplaying something. The waiter returned with the drinks causing them both to pause for a moment. After he left they returned to the conversation. Randy had heard about Enoch being on the news, and also knew it had something to do with whatever had happened to those officers. Randy didn't want any parts of that business, and wasn't sure if the lash he had put Enoch onto was connected in any way. Enoch sat across from him locking eyes as he sipped his drink; hat pulled low with designer glasses on he could tell Enoch was trying to hide his identity.

"I see you made the news my nigga. You are a very popular man to be on so many segments." Enoch's eyes kind of went wide showing his surprise at the comment Randy had just made. He took his time to regain his composure before saying anything.

"Yeah unfortunate events that I pray clear themselves up. I keep to many irons on the fire and one happened to get a little too hot. Nothing for you to worry about, just a circumstantial matter."

Randy liked hearing that. Even though he put Enoch up on the lick and allowed the club to be used as a prop, he was not about that life. No way was he willing to sacrifice all he had worked for.

"Well I hope all goes well on that end of your business. Is Karter okay?" Randy asked.

"Yeah she good, I wouldn't be here with you now if she wasn't!" Enoch responded. Randy just nodded his head up and down in understanding. He picked up one of his drinks and took a large gulp...

****

"Hello sir, welcome to Tomfooleries what can I do for you?" Drako with his Blue K.C. hat on, sat at the bar appearing to be alone. He wanted a drink but wasn't sure the bartender would serve him one, so for the sake of wanting maintain a low profile he just ordered a cheeseburger skillet pizza and a large sprite. He sat there looking at all those assorted bottles of alcohol mouthwatering. He diverted his attention to the television above the display, he was willing to try anything to calm his nerves. He pulled a cigarette out of his jacket pocket and fired it up.

Whatever the program that was on the television was interrupted by a news flash. When Drako saw a news reporter standing on the corner with the backdrop showing the Dodge Challenger being lifted onto a flatbed tow truck it instantly got his undivided attention. He couldn't hear what was being reported so he asked the bartender to turn up the television. "Multiple officers dead and wounded in a shootout that happened not to far from here. The police were trying to apprehend the passengers in this vehicle you see here behind me due to its connection to the shooting deaths of the officers at the Belton Inn Motel."

"Enoch Jackson is the man who is being sought after as a person of question connected to these shootings. The police still are not sure what part he may have played in any of today's events, but consider him armed and dangerous. They want you to call tips hotline if you have any information concerning this man or today's events." Drako just sat there eyes glossy. One reason being seeing that scene again with the car caused him to see his boy lying dead in the backseat eyes staring at nothing. He was also feeling confused and betrayed by Enoch.

How could he give him that car knowing it was hot as a firecracker? Is this why the laws jumped down on him and his crew like that? Did they expect to find Enoch behind the wheel? Did Enoch know all this when he came and traded him cars? Was he looking for someone solid to take his downfall? The bartender placed his pizza and drink down in front of him bringing him out of his reverie.

Drako snapped back to reality, thanked the man for his order and told him it would be okay to bring him his bill. He tore into the pizza, one cause he was hungry. two cause he needed to put his attention on something else to clear his mind. It didn't take him long to finish the pizza so he sat there pretending to

watch the television while nursing his sprite. He was working on his second one when he saw Enoch and the man he was sitting in the booth with get up and leave through the reflection of the large mirror behind the bar. He did as he was told counted to 200 before getting up to leave behind them...
****

Enoch and Randy were walking towards the covered parking garage on the lower level.

"Man those drinks must have ran right straight through a nigga!" Enoch said. He looked back toward the restaurant as if he was thinking about going back in.

"Man you better go piss behind one of these cars!" Randy responded with a drunk chuckle. They both noticed the young man walking across the street behind them but didn't give him much thought due to him walking towards the entrance to the upper levels.

Enoch took Randy's advice and continued to walk in to the covered garage. As soon as he got into the entrance he walked behind the first row of cars to relieve himself. After about a minute Randy wondered what was taking him so long asked him, "What you over there doing nigga taking a shit?" He dug into his pockets and pulled out his pack of cigarettes, fired one up and continued to wait on Enoch. After about two drags Enoch came back from behind the cars walking kinda wobbly.

"Took you long enough nigga! Let's get the fuck up outta here before one of these good Samaritan ass white folks call the police thinking we trying to steal a car."

Enoch just laughed at Randy's comment. "You right nigga, that's a mishap I can't afford to happen down here on this Country Club Plaza!" They walked to Enoch's car and both hopped in. Enoch gave Randy a brown paper sack with the money inside of it. Randy opened the bag and checked its contents. Satisfied by what he saw he smiled at Enoch and gave him a pound.

"Where you park at my nigga? I will pull you right up to the Rover so you won't have to walk."

"I'm on the upper level my nigga." Randy told him.

Enoch put the Mustang in gear and proceeded to drive Randy where he wanted to go. Enoch pulled right in front of Randy's red Range Rover and told him to get at him when he had something else up for him. Randy assured him that he would, gave Enoch another pound, and hopped out heading to his truck. Enoch rode off before he got in which made Randy expel a breath of relief. He wasn't sure he was going to get a dime from Enoch and felt better seeing Enoch didn't try to fuck him.

He hit the keypad to unlock his doors feeling better with every step he took. He opened the door to the Range rover and felt something tap his leg just as he was about to hop in. He kinda jumped and looked down right into the barrel of a Glock 40. He never even got to convey a thought before three shots went off, two entered right under his chin exiting through the top of his skull. The last shot missed him entirely due to the fact that he was already falling backwards. Drako rolled from under the truck, grabbed the bag as well keys that had fallen to the ground with Randy, hopped into the driver's seat of the Range Rover, and pulled away like nothing had even happened...

Drako was driving the Range Rover as if he were the owner. He had just put his murder game down and felt satisfied with the outcome. In the vicious streets of Killa City you had to always be prepared to be what was needed to be at the drop of a dime. While driving east on 47th St. leaving the plaza he pulled over to the side of the road and tossed the Glock 40 in the gutter. He had come across a 9mm Ruger P89 with an extended 30 round clip inside the console of the Range Rover.

No way was he willing to take the chance on getting caught with a murder weapon when he no longer needed it. Now he needed luck to continue to be on his side hoping to make it to the rendezvous spot him and Enoch had agreed upon with no mishaps. He continued to ride down 47th St in silence thinking about today's events and how they had unfolded.

He was still in pain about his boys, Dink and Tre. The shit he saw on the news still had him fucked up also. How could the Big Homie put them in that position without first warning them? Drako wasn't sure if the police jumped down on them like that cause of Enoch, him and his crew had plenty of reasons why it could have been them the police were looking for. He just couldn't get past the feeling that Enoch should have at least put them up on game.

He was finally now pulling into the carwash off Eastwood Trafficway and wasn't surprised to see the Mustang sitting inside one of the stalls. He pulled the Range Rover into the stall next to it, grabbed the bag of money as well as the P89, hopped out the truck and went and hopped in the passenger seat of the Mustang. The car was filled with the sweet smell of the kush Enoch had just finished smoking. He was now snorting lines of cocaine off of the owner's manual of the Mustang, as soon as Drako shut the door he passed him the makeshift plate. Drako took the offer and snorted two lines up both nostrils.

"I see things went as planned." Enoch said. Drako couldn't answer right off due to him having his head tilted back attempting to catch the drain from the coke. He eventually just looked over at Enoch and just nodded his head. He couldn't speak yet cause the coke kind of had him froze. Enoch handed him a cup with some alcohol he had been drinking so he could clear his throat. Drako took a couple of gulps handed the cup back feeling a little better.

He looked in the backseat and didn't see his AR-15 so he looked over at the floorboard area of the driver's side of the car. Enoch recognizing what he had to be looking for eased his worries. "I put it in the trunk before I went in the restaurant. Couldn't afford to have some good Samaritan see it and have the laws on me as I was coming out. You know how those white people on the plaza get down!" Drako just shook his head that he understood the move and his reasoning. Drako now finally able to speak had questions for Enoch.

"Aye Bro you know I saw you on the news while we were in there?"

"Word?" was all Enoch said in response.

"Yeah, showed your picture and everything. Said something about wanting you in connection of with some downed cops out south."

"I ain't sweating that shit little homie. The question is what are you now going to do since you got you some bread in your hands?"

"I really don't know. Without my team I am a sitting duck for the suckas as well as the police. I may have to shake the scene for a while." Drako wasn't trusting Enoch due to his inability to show emotion for what he had just told him.

In his mind who could have things so figured out when dead cops were involved. Enoch had also just had him knock a nigga he had supposed to be doing business with. Drako was sure if he hadn't of happened to call Enoch and been with him at the time he would have put the work in himself. Shit, knowing Enoch he probably still wishes he had, so he could have kept the money for himself. Drako's thoughts were interrupted by Enoch's voice.

"Where do you want me to take you and your newfound wealth my nigga?"

"Shit for now you can just drop me over my little bitches crib in The Citadel." Drako told him.

"Cool." was all Enoch said as he was putting the mustang in gear.

"Hold up big homie we can't be riding around town with the chop in the trunk like that!"

"You damn right we can't little homie!" Enoch said as he put the mustang back in park, hit the trunk pop button, and hopped out to go retrieve the gun from the trunk. Enoch was back with the gun in hand in like 30 seconds.

He handed it to Drako across the seat, hopped in, and proceeded to put the Mustang in gear. Pop Pop Pop Pop!!! Four shots from the Ruger hit Enoch right in the right side of his chest. Instantly he slumped against the steering wheel no longer moving. Drako now with the smoking gun in his pocket hopped out the Mustang, AR-15 in one hand, brown bag in the other. He walked back to the Range Rover, hopped in, started it up, and rode out of the parking lot headed straight for the highway...

Chapter 27

Karter awoke from her sleep with a jolt. She looked over at the bedside stand at the alarm clock and noticed it was only 12:00 A.M. After being up most of the night before she knew she should have at least slept through the night. The medication Keisha went and got for her at the pharmacy still had her kind of woozy, but she was sure she was awoken from her sleep because something was wrong. She kicked off the covers, crawled out of bed, and went to use the bathroom.

After relieving herself she went downstairs to see if something was amiss. Upon reaching the bottom of the stairs she ran into Jay letting someone out the door. From the looks of the tattered rags the man was wearing that were supposed to be clothes she could tell he was there to buy crack. Jay shut the door behind the man and asked her was she good, she assured him that she was fine. She walked over and plopped down right in the middle of the couch.

Jay just looked at her wondering what made her think he wasn't already sitting there. Karter immediately read his vibe and said, "I am sorry Jay were you sitting here?"

"Nah I just had Carlitos Way playing on Netflix, blunt half smoked in the ashtray, with my beer right there on the table for no reason!" Jay snapped back.

Karter laughed at his sarcasm and scooted over out of the way. Jay watched her she as she did so and noticed her wince slightly, this made him feel bad for making her move from his spot.

"Jay, can I use your phone please?" Karter asked him.

"Lil Sis you know better, that is something you don't even have to ask!" He grabbed his phone off of the table and handed it to her.

"I have one more favor to ask." Karter said in her little girl voice.

"Spill it Karter, you fucking with my vibe now!" Jay said in an aggressive yet playful tone.

"I need you to go get Enoch's number out of Keisha's phone please?" Jay just looked at Karter for like 10 seconds like she was crazy.

"Karter wouldn't it have been easier for you to have just walked over to Keisha's room and fuck up her vibe?"

Karter laughed at Jays remark, she knew what he said made all the sense, but she wasn't aware of what she wanted to do before she instinctively made her way down the stairs.

"Jay please, I promise not to bother you anymore."

Jay expelled a breath of exaggerated frustration, got up, and went to get Keisha's phone. He was there and back in no time, he handed Karter the phone and got back to his movie. Karter used Keisha's phone and tried the number she had talked to Enoch on earlier. The phone rang and rang in here ear with no answer on the other end. Karter tried again with the same results, she ended the call feeling a sense of fear she had never felt before. She sat there knowing something was wrong with no explanation as to why. Enoch was out there in trouble; this was something she was sure of.

She used Keisha's phone and went to the Channel 5 news app. The latest story on the news feed was the report of the shooting involving officers on 42nd and Wabash. She saw the car in the backdrop of the report and dropped the phone to the floor. Her eyes welled up with tears due to the fact that she felt that the law either had her man or he was dead. Jay looked over at her while he was smoking the rest of his blunt. "You okay little sis?" Karter didn't even acknowledge that she had heard him, she just sat there with her feet pulled under her, silently crying for her boo...

Karter stopped her sniffles when she heard the front door open and in walks Kelly. Bags in hand from the various stores she had been shopping at earlier in the day. After closing the door behind her she sat the bags down on the floor, she sashayed across the room heading directly for the kitchen. She walked right past Karter and Jay sitting on the couch as if she didn't even see them sitting there, no acknowledgments or anything. Kelly was rude like that, she acted as if her shit didn't stink, or her pussy didn't bleed once a month like every other female in the world.

She returned from the kitchen, cup of juice now in hand, and plopped her ass down right between Jay and Karter without saying "excuse me" or anything else that would have shown that she had home training. Jay just looked at her like she was crazy as he scooted over to make room on the couch for Kelly's ample ass. She saw Karter sitting there silently crying, tears falling down her face and decided to pretend to be concerned, "Karter are you okay?" Karter didn't even acknowledge that she even heard her so she looked over at Jay as if he may have been the culprit.

Jay didn't even let on that he felt her staring a hole in the side of his face, per Keisha's directions he had mastered the art of not paying Kelly any attention. This made Kelly suspicious, so she turned her body towards Karter, left leg on the couch, back now to Jay, looking to get to the bottom of what had her cousin so upset. Jay took this as his cue to leave, knowing he would now never finish his movie in peace, he gathered his things and went upstairs to him and Keisha's room.

"Karter... Karter, what is going on, what is wrong with you?" Kelly asked her again. Karter just looked through Kelly as if she didn't even see her, looking as if she was possessed. Kelly was really worried now being that she had never saw her cousin like this before. She leaned forward and just wrapped her arms around Karter tears now falling down her face also. After a while of this Karter said one word so soft Kelly could barely hear it, "Enoch."

This shook Kelly, so she just looked into Karter's eyes looking for a meaning behind the word. Did Karter know about what happened earlier? Had her deceit been the cause of her cousin's mood? Kelly couldn't take another minute of whatever it was so she got up from the couch, went and grabbed her bags, and climbed the stairs heading to the room where her dirty deed with Enoch had been done. Karter just sat there like that crying until she went to sleep right there on the couch.

Chapter 28

Present day

"*B*ITCH, stop spraying that fucking water in my face!"

As I was attempting to lather up during a much needed makeshift shower, my female captor kept spraying the water from the hose in my face. I am sure days have passed as I stand here trying to get this funky smell off of my body. I was starting to function better under the influence of whatever drug my captors have been pumping me up with. I was given a large dose before being unhooked from the chain, and marched to the opposite side of the cellar for a shower I am now receiving.

With nothing but a rag and a bottle of body wash, I am washing myself as best I possibly can with my hands cuffed. I have been searching my surroundings every possible chance I get for a weapon to wield so I can attempt an escape. The keys as well as a small handgun are in the jacket pocket of my female captor. The male is still the one who feeds me, as well as drug me up. But for this job he allows "She Devil", as I have named her, to hold the reigns.

She hasn't spoken a word to me but seems intent on terrorizing me every time the opportunity presents itself. The last time my male captor allowed her down here with me alone, it was to empty my stool bucket. The evil bitch tipped it over on the end of the mattress with an exaggerated "oops". I want to take my chances and rush the bitch, but I plan to live through the ordeal and being shot doesn't seem like a smart way to ensure this happens.

I have been regaining my strength by doing calisthenics as soon as they drug me up and go upstairs. I work up a good sweat to get as much of the drug out of my system as possible. This mixed with the fact that my tolerance has risen helps me stay coherent longer each day. My captors have yet to ask me for anything or tell me why I am here, so I am convinced that this is the torture phase.

I hear them talking amongst themselves sometimes, but I can't make out what's being said or who the voices belong to. I also hear a baby crying from time to time. This is what really has be baffled cause for the life of me I can't remember having any dealings with a couple who was expecting. Suddenly my captor stops spraying the water on me, leaving me covered in soap from my neck to my feet.

I just stand there looking at her wondering what's the hold up. "Times up bitch!" she says. I just stand there looking at my body then at her, watching soap suds run down my body. "If you want your towel, clothes or to be fed; you would be trying to hurry up and get over in your area so I can put your dawg ass back on your chain!" she says. I want to rush this bitch so bad, but I am buying my time. She doesn't know that I am not as weak as she presumes me to be; she doesn't know that I plan to bust that ass as soon as the opportunity presents itself.

I start walking towards her causing her to drop the hose and grab her gun out of her pocket and point it directly at my face. "Bitch don't get ya brains blown out for playing games with me!" I just veered off course and returned to my little cubby hole, picked up the bath towel off the mattress and dried the soapy water off my body. It took my captor almost two seconds to remove that gun from her pocket and get it into a position to fire.

When the time was right, two seconds would be more than enough time for me to get on her ass and regain my freedom. I just had to keep myself alert and ready, as well as make note of the schedule my captors kept. After getting dressed into the cheap cotton sweat suit they had given me, I was made to lie down with my hands stretched above my head, so she could refasten my cuffs to the chain.

After she went upstairs my male captor came down with food, water and my daily dosage of whatever it was they had been pumping me up with. After he drugged me up this time, my captor didn't leave like had usually been doing. I laid there on the mattress with my eyes closed, fighting the effects of the drug pretending to be out of it. I felt the mattress shift, alerting me to him being in close proximity.

I slowed my breathing attempting to appear to be out of it. I felt a tickling sensation, like something was crawling on me around my neck and shoulder area. As it proceeded up my neck towards my face I realized that it was his gloved finger. He stroked the top of my neck before moving on to my ears, then my mouth, following up with my nose. It was hard for me to stay awake at this point due to the effects of the drug.

He took his finger and circled both of my eyes before drawing a heart with his fingertip between my eyebrows. My eyes popped open in shock causing him to reflectivity snatch back his hand. I was now staring him eye to eye not believing what I thought I was seeing. There was only one man who had ever touched me like that and it was impossible for him to be here kneeling perched over me.

He just stared right back at me smiling from behind the mask as the drugs finally had their desired effect and took me under. Once again I was riding with Enoch not understanding why I had taken him back.

Chapter 29

*E*noch came back to consciousness with a jolt, he was disoriented and in excruciating pain. He was having trouble inhaling due to the impact from the gunshots. He slowly came back to reality, playing back the last moments he could remember in his head. He remembered getting the gun out of the trunk for Drako, getting back inside the car, and the gunshots. He checked the car over and realized that there were no bullet holes inside the car and the glass from all the windows was still intact.

That confused him until he realized that Drako was no longer inside the car with him. He moved to take his jacket off to check himself for injuries. He noticed that there was no blood on the outside of his clothes and wanted to be sure that his bulletproof vest didn't get penetrated. Drako had tried to kill him for reasons he couldn't quite figure out at the moment, but he would worry about that later.

He winced as he managed to get his jacket off as well as well the shirt he was wearing under it. He unstrapped the bulletproof vest and took that off as well. He turned on the overhead light in the Mustang and saw four large circular bruises on his chest. Just seeing them made him take a moment to thank the Creator for sparing his life.

He picked up his cellphone and realized that he had missed a few calls from Sis, he felt that he couldn't worry about that right now being that he had to get himself out of this carwash and somewhere safe. He tossed the vest into the passenger seat, awkwardly put his shirt back on, took his bag of coke out of his pocket and with a rolled up bill and took to two toots straight from the bag.

He instantly felt a little better with the coke rushing through his bloodstream, taking away the pain. He then dialed a number and after about five rings his call was answered.

"Hello!"

"Baby I am on my way to you." was all that was needed to be said by Enoch.

"Okay." before anything else was allowed to be said Enoch ended the call and tossed the phone onto the passenger seat. He put the Mustang in gear and pulled out into the late night traffic, finally headed home after a long 24 hours.

****

3910 East 56th St. is the address of the home of Karren Brown and her son Enoch Nasir Jackson Jr. The fact that she lived in Friendship Village one of Killa City's most notorious housing projects wasn't her downfall, being the girlfriend of Enoch was. She was young, pretty, and driven but also ratchet, easily controlled, and naive.

She had been with Enoch off and on since high school at his convenience. She loved how he would hit the streets to provide her with the finer things in life. Jewelry, clothes, her Nissan Maxima, as well as trips across the country. It wasn't as if she couldn't take care of herself, she had been working as a registered nurse for the last three years. Enoch had never asked her to do anything out of the ordinary for these extra things other than remain faithful to him when he wasn't around.

His first and only time going to jail, she visited faithfully from his time spent in the county jail all the way to "The Walls" prison where he did his time in Jefferson City for 3 1\2 years. As of right now he hadn't been home in at least two weeks, but she was sure that whenever he got home he would also have the bag secured. She knew not to sweat him unless she wanted to get a taste of his violent side; after being smacked around more than once over the years she knew exactly what to do to prevent this from happening.

She liked the arrangement, with him being gone so much this gave her all the time she needed to drop her son off over her mothers and go gallivanting around the city. Two could play the games he played if you asked her, what he didn't know couldn't hurt him.

Karren got her shit off whenever Enoch left her for so long, her itch just had to be scratched. One of those times her getting scratched left her with more of an itch than what she was looking for.

Enoch had been away on one of his longer stays running the streets, which was good cause it gave Karren just enough time to get rid of her itch. The front door opened and in walks Enoch visibly in pain from the way he was walking. Karren was just coming from the kitchen preparing her a plate of last night's leftovers, when she saw that Enoch appeared to be hurt and dropped her plate on the floor right where she stood.

She ran over and helped escort him to the couch. "Baby what happened to you?" she asked him. Enoch just looked at her with a look like he was constipated while lying back on the couch. Karren asked him again "Enoch what happened? Are you okay?" "Bitch do it look like I am okay? Help me take this shirt off and then go run me a hot bath!" Karren did exactly as she was told, helping Enoch get the shirt over his head while he winced in pain.

When the shirt was off Karren saw the marks on Enoch's chest and started to cry. "Bitch what are you standing there crying for? What you need to be doing in checking my ribs for breaks or cracks. I thought this was the type of shit you saw all the time?" Karren wiped the tears from her eyes, then went about the business of tenderly probing Enoch's chest with her fingers. When she didn't feel any noticeable breaks she left Enoch lying on the couch and went in the bathroom to start the water for his bath.

When she came back in the room Enoch had got himself up into a sitting position and was leaning over the coffee table snorting lines of coke. She just looked at him shook her head and started to clean up the mess from the dropped plate. After finishing with that, she grabbed Enoch's guns and took them to put them up out of reach in the bedroom. The water was finished running by this time so she shut it off, came back into the front room to get Enoch and help him undress and get in the tub.

Every fiber of her being told her to undress and get in the tub with him but she knew this was not the time. Enoch just laid in the tub and allowed the water to engulf his whole body. Karren just sat on the toilet and watched him as he appeared to fall asleep in the water. This was the first time she had ever saw him hurt, and it had just come to her that he wasn't invincible.

What would she tell their son if something terrible were to happen to his father? How would she make it without him? These questions as well as other fears ran through Karren's mind nonstop. Just when she was sure he had fallen asleep, he asked her to help wash him. Karren thought he would never ask and was disappointed when this was really all he wanted. She helped him out the tub. When she was done she dried him off, and helped walk him to the bedroom, naked as the day he was born.

She put him in the bed beside their sleeping son and pulled the comforter up to his chin. Enoch was asleep almost as soon as he hit the bed, the long day had given him all he could handle. Karren went back to the front room turned out the lights, cleaned up Enoch's mess, and returned to the bedroom. She hopped in the bed on the other side of their son, said a silent prayer, then went to sleep herself...

Chapter 30

Agent Jones stood at the podium in front of the room of the joint task force, undeniably in a very bad mood. It had been two weeks since the hotel shooting and not one lead had been produced by any of the departments involved in the investigation. This was the third time they all had met at the downtown police department and Agent Jones was starting to feel like they all were wasting his time.

Today he felt like returning the favor in kind, he would have them all sit here while he took them step by step with what they already knew and didn't know. "We have at least three Un-Subs from the Belton Inn shooting that we have yet to find a lead on. We have Enoch Jackson as our person of interest whom we have yet to even get a tip as to his whereabouts. We are almost sure he wasn't one of the shooters at the Belton Inn, but we still aren't sure how he is involved. The deceased Un-Sub had tattoos that our intelligence has confirmed connects him to the Mexican Mafia."

"We can thank California department of Corrections for that information, as well as the extra info on how this gang operates. We have a list of subjects with ties to this gang that we believe are to be operating in this area, but we haven't been able to tie one of them to the crimes committed in this investigation. Matter of fact we have yet to apprehend anyone to even be able to interrogate them. We have the last known address for Enoch Jackson, which is 3815 Chestnut. The owner of the property is one Shirley Stevens AKA Bunny. She has 3 priors 2 for minor theft charges and one minor possession."

"She has had a clean record for the last twenty years and isn't cooperating much. She says she hasn't seen him in at least a month and won't let us search the house without a warrant. The judge assigned to this case is not willing to give us a warrant based on what we have alone. The Dodge Challenger was pretty much clean despite the body we found in the backseat from a gunshot wound to the head. Ballistics show it was shots fired by one of the officers involved in the attempted arrest that claimed his life."

"We do have a DNA analysis from the van we impounded from the Belton Inn shooting. The blood appears to have come from two different Un-Subs. We have no matches for these samples in our database, but we can attempt to find the match if and when we catch up with those who are responsible."
Ozzy happened to walk in late as usual with his team trailing behind him. Agent Jones not one to let an

opportunity like this to pass pounced right on Ozzy like a hungry lion.

"Agent Jablowski, so glad you could make it. We are all just sitting here going over what we do and don't have. Is there anything at this point that you would like to add to either one of these lists?" Agent Jablowski stopped in his tracks while the rest of his team continued to file into the room and find seating in the last available chairs. He took about ten seconds pretending to read all of what Agent Jones had written on the power point projector.

One more person entered the room who Agent Jones wasn't familiar with, she walked over and stood next to Ozzy while he pretended to be interested by what he was reading. Ozzy knew that the suspense was killing Agent Jones. He could tell by the look on his face that he was puzzled as to who this woman was standing here next to him and also if he had anything to add as far as leads or evidence pertaining to the case.

"Agent Jablowski, we are waiting!" Ozzy just stood there a couple more seconds before finally giving in.

"I am sorry Jonsey about my punctuality, I understand how important the work we are all attempting to do here is and I by no means meant to come in and be a disruption. I had to pick up Special Agent Simpson from the airport. I will now allow her to introduce herself as well as explain why she is here." Agent Jones just stood there silent. He was fuming now cause Agent Jablowski had called him by his nickname in front of all these people.

He decided that he would be patient and see what Agent Simpson had to say before he went off the handle. "Agent Jones would you mind stepping up here to the front and introducing yourself? If there is a special reason you are here we would all love to hear that also." Agent Simpson outfitted in a severe black business suit with a cream colored blouse made her way to the front of the room. Her legs were very well toned which seemed to be holding the attention of all the men who had the advantage point to catch a glimpse. Her high heeled tan pumps made a clacking sound with each step she took.

She was a beautiful woman who never had a problem gaining a man's attention, it's just that in her profession the attention she sometimes got wasn't always attached to the respect she demanded. She had graduated Summa Cum Laude from M.I.T. and knew her shit. She was a member of the F.B.I.'s supreme genius division. She was here because it was her that had easily figured out how to get closer to some answers that they all had been chasing for weeks.

When she got to the podium Agent Jones instinctively moved out of her way giving her the floor. "Hello my name is Special Agent Sandra

Simpson and I am a member of the supreme genius squad stationed in Washington D.C. I am here because Agent Ohashi sent us the tracking device that was found hidden in the money retrieved from the scene of the crime. I wish she would have done so earlier because it took me no longer than a couple hours to track the digital fingerprint back to its original position." She continued.

"By using Google Maps we have an address for where the tracker was first activated. It sat there for a very long period of time so I believe this is the location the money was originally stored at. I also figured out what service was used for the activation, but there is no name on the account. I took it upon myself to go to my superiors in Washington with the results of my findings in order to fast track us obtaining a no knock warrant for the address in which is in question.

"We have been watching the location via satellite and there has been minimal traffic in and out of the residence. All the cars we have spotted have been luxury and seem to belong to who's ever residence this is. We don't know who's driving these cars or how many people may be riding in them due to the fact that they always pull into the garage. We only have so much time that we were able to surveil the property cause of cloud cover and the earth's rotation. When we go in we are pretty much going in blind. We don't know how many people may be inside, if they may be armed, or if there are be any children living at this residence."

"I am not in charge here, but I express the fact that my superiors in Washington expect for you all to be very professional and cautious. This house is in a very influential neighborhood and the press would have a field day with us if any innocent bystanders happened to be harmed by a stray bullet. The last thing any of our departments need is to be fighting lawsuits instead of crime. Now that I am finished I will turn the floor back over to Special Agent Jones." Agent Simpson ended.

Agent Jones stepped back to the podium, he took a moment looking over the written reports as well as the warrant Agent Simpson had left on the podium. "1075 Tam-Oshanter Dr., are any of you familiar with this area? I want a task force put together with six officers a apiece from all three of our departments. I want this done within the hour. I need someone to find us an architectural layout of the house, so we won't be totally blind. I know we are all emotionally involved in this so please have your heads on straight and use every precaution possible."

"This is our only lead we can't fuck this up. I will leave it up to you all to figure out who goes and who doesn't, I only ask that these decisions be made quickly and confidently. We will meet at the command vehicle which will be parked the on 31st St Bridge, in-between Woodland and Brooklyn. From there we will all take the highway straight to our destination. Ladies and gentlemen we have a lot riding on this one let's be professional and responsible, I'll see you there."

The hustle and bustle of the room was very amplified. There wasn't an officer in the room who didn't want to be involved in this raid. It was finally time for some retribution for their comrades who had fallen in the line of duty. All of them knew it wouldn't be possible to be involved so they all shared the energy that would be needed for whomever it was that was chosen. They were going to kick a door down, and whoever was on the other side had better have the answers they so desperately had been trying to get for two weeks now...

Chapter 31

*L*ittle Enoch shrieked and laughed as his daddy crawled on his knees chasing him barking like a dog. The chase led them to the kitchen where Little Enoch was now attempting to hide under his mothers' skirt as she stood at the counter washing the dishes. Enoch lunged at his son causing him to bump his head on the door of the cabinet. Instantly his laughter turned to cries of pain, causing his momma to stop what she was doing so she could pick him up and console him. Enoch seeing the game was over got up to his feet and walked over to help.

"Ah little nigga you aight, quit crying!" Karren just stood there with Little Enoch in her arms bouncing him and rubbing the back of his head. "You keep babying that little nigga like that and he is sure to grow up to be a bitch. He only crying like that because he knows how you are going to react. When you at work he knows not to even try me like that, cause he would be crying until you got home!"

Karren just stood there lookin at Enoch like he was crazy, he was standing in front of her, shirt off, ribs and chest wrapped like the mummy. He had been here at her house without leaving for the last two weeks recovering from the injuries sustained the night he arrived. She was happy to have him here with his son, and even though she enjoyed his company she couldn't wait for him to hit the streets. The injuries he had sustained had pretty much healed, but he seemed to now have a new ailment.

He had run out of coke a few days after he had got here, the pain he was in caused him to snort a lot more than usual. He needed something for the pain so he gave Karren money to cop him some Percocet's, and OxyContin from her home girl that worked at the pharmacy. He had been eating those pills like candy for almost two weeks now and Karren was no longer convinced that he was eating them for just the pain.

At first the pills were giving him fits while he slept due to the nightmares they caused him to have. He now would nod off and you couldn't tell if he was alive or dead until he woke from his temporary coma. His moods were starting to become unpredictable and violent. He had recently just smacked the shift out of Karren for what he believed was her talking about him to one of her friends on the phone. He knew the police was looking for him and didn't want her telling anybody that he may happen to be here at her apartment. The little bit of cash he had left was sure to run out soon if he kept going at this pace.

He only had one of the $5,000 knots and close to $7,500 he had taken from Jokers Goons in his pockets when he first arrived here at Karren's. Enoch gave Karren $5,000 for her and his son as soon as he woke up the day after his arrival. He had been chunking out of the $7,500 for the meds, and they weren't cheap on the black market. His being cooped up in the house was starting to take its toll on him. He was worried about Karter and Sis, as well as the work he had left them with.

He didn't want them believing he had flew the coop and left them with that shit to keep for themselves. His phone had been powered off since the first night. He knew Karter was blowing his shit up once she figured out that he wasn't dead or in jail.

"Boy what's wrong with you standing there all spaced out and shit?" Enoch snapped back to reality and just stared and Karren like she was crazy.

"You need to stop taking those pills, they are starting to fuck with your mind!" She told him.

"Bitch you got me fucked up! Enoch stronger than anything man can make. What's fucking with my mind is being cooped up in this crib with your basic ass! If you ain't trying to dope me up so I can bang your back out, you are coddling that little nigga like you are doing right now. How is a nigga supposed to stay sane under these conditions?" Karren just stood there staring at Enoch giving him the evil eye.

She wanted to say something so bad, but her mind was telling her that he was right. Karren was used to the abuse and it kept her from seeing what the truth really was. This nigga was not good for her or her son.

"Right bitch, nothing to say huh?" The last strand of restraint broke and Karren let it all out.

"Bang my back out??? Nigga you can barely even hang, minute man! I have to catch you under the influence cause clearly otherwise it seems like you be wanting to be somewhere else. You treat a bitch like she is less than dirt. You haven't been the same since you got out of prison. Would you rather I was some young boy? Are you sure you wouldn't rather have your dick in some niggas ass?"

Before she could finish her rant Enoch had took two good strides across the kitchen and smacked the shit out Karren. She flew up against the sink, letting her son go, causing him to fall into the dishwater in the sink. Seeing this didn't even slow Enoch down for a second, he followed with a left hook from his closed fist.

"Bitch you done lost your mind disrespecting me like that!" Pop Pop Pop. Enoch kept smacking Karren as she slid to the floor, back propped up against the cabinets.

"Bitch you think I don't know you got some secret nigga?" Pop Pop! "Bitch is this why you think you gone disrespect me like I am some lame?" He yelled.

All while Little Enoch is standing calf deep in dishwater crying his eyes out. Enoch was now in a rage, he was now smacking the shit out of Karren who had now went limp and was laying sprawled out on the floor. Little Enoch saw what was happening to his momma and tried to get out of the sink to come to her aid. While holding on the side of the sink he put his right leg over the side in an attempt to get out of the water.

With nowhere for his foot to find placement he flipped right out of the sink, falling to the floor landing on his back. He let out a wail so loud it brought Enoch back to his senses. He looked at his son then at Karren who was now bleeding from a cut on her eye as well as her mouth. He was still angry but now at himself for the destruction he had brought to his safe haven. This was supposed to be his refuge, his place to get away from it all. His mind now in overdrive he proceeded to gather all his things so he could make his exit. He wasn't sure who may have heard them or if Karren would want to call the law on him.

He was now in Karren's room putting the guns as well as his phone in his sons' book bag. He hastily got dressed, grabbed the rest of his pills out of the bedside nightstand, as well as his car keys. Just as he was closing the drawer Karren came in the room crying.

"What are you doing? You think you just gone leave us here like this?" Enoch looked at her and was instantly ashamed at the damage he had caused. His heart was breaking with every beat which is why he knew he had to get out of here.

"Baby I am sorry, but since I am such a burden to you I must get out of here. I have clearly overstayed my welcome."

"No please don't go! I am sorry I didn't mean it." Karren managed to get out in between cries.

Little Enoch had finally made it up the stairs and walked in the room still crying. This was all Enoch could take, one look at his son and the realization for who and what he was pushed him over the edge. He just looked at them both as Karren picked up their son.

"I am sorry but I have to go. I love you both too much to attempt to stay."

With that being said he left out the door back into the streets. Karren heard the door close and sat down on the bed with her son crying. Although she wanted her space she wasn't sure how much space her words may have gotten her. She attacked his manhood so she may no longer have a man, only time would tell. She had a million thoughts going through her head about the possibilities while lying there with her son.

Eventually her thoughts and her tears were too much, so her and her son just laid in the bed and cried themselves to sleep.

Chapter 32

*K*arter was ripping up the road in her new whip. She had used part of the cash Enoch had left for her to cop a brand new Chevy Camaro, and she was loving how the 6.2 liter V8 engine handled the roads. Riding through the city listening to Miseducation of Lauryn Hill had her vibing and missing Enoch. Karter had been missing him as well as worried about him. She knew he wasn't in jail cause periodically the news would flash his picture calling him Kansas City's most wanted. Karter had also heard about the death of Randy and how he was found dead in a parking garage on the Country Club Plaza.

Knowing that Randy was the one who put her and Enoch on their latest caper, she was sure Enoch had something to do with his death. Enoch didn't believe in leaving loose ends, if he felt that Randy was one then he was sure to take care of him. Thankfully the news only spoke of him being found murdered but didn't have any leads. The city was talking about adding surveillance cameras cause people no longer felt safe in one of the city's more affluent shopping districts.

Karter just wanted to make it out of the last ordeal unscathed. She was no longer pregnant and this was both a relief and a disappointment. She wanted to keep the baby but the reality was she was strung out and made a living in the streets. How could she bring a child into this world under those conditions.

She was sure this was a life she no longer wanted to live. She knew that she had more to offer to this world than tricking and robbing niggas. She knew Enoch wouldn't be trying to hear this, but she now had a little change of her own to venture out and try something new. She pulled into a parking spot in Keisha's house where she had been staying lately. She dug into her purse, took out her fix bag, tapped out some coke on the spot between her thumb and pointer finger and snorted it off.

Her habit was getting worse due to her anxiety. She needed to see Enoch so she could clear a lot of her fears from her mind. She didn't want anyone to know that she had started snorting coke. It was hard enough defending the relationship she shared with Enoch without giving extra ammunition to anyone who wanted to see her leave him alone. To Karter her two addictions were better than the ones she witnessed other people struggle with.

Keisha and her man like to sell the shit just as much as she liked snorting it. These last few weeks she had saw them making money hand over fist.

Karter got out of her car and retrieved her bags from shopping and made her way to the apartment. She saw a Mustang parked a few cars down that she had never saw before and spent a few seconds admiring it. She finally made it to the door, used her key to gain entry and damn near fainted when she saw Enoch sitting on the couch drinking beers and smoking weed with Jay.

She dropped her bags on the floor and just stood there staring at him with a big ass smile on her face. Enoch and Jay both turned and were looking at her like she was crazy. "Damn you trying to let all the flys in too?" Jay knew she was happy to see her man but he couldn't allow an opportunity to rub her face in it to get by. "Take a picture it will last longer." Keisha walked into the room with a glass of wine laughing at Jays smart remarks aimed towards Karter.

"Boy leave her alone. You know she's happy to F-I-N-A-L-L-Y see her man." Keisha said with extra exaggeration on the finally. Karter finally shut the door feeling a little embarrassed by her reaction. She walked over and grabbed Enoch by his head pulling it backwards over the back of the couch and laid a wet nasty kiss right on his mouth. "Either you two go and get a room or I am about to pull out my phone and start recording." Jay teased.

Karter broke the kiss and just looked at Jay with a big ass smile on her face. Keisha popped Jay upside his head, told him to come on and made her way up the stairs. Jay acting like he was reluctant to follow. Finally, he did as he was told once he saw Keisha standing on the stairs waiting on him. He grabbed his beer and followed, with the blunt they were smoking hanging out of his mouth. Karter flipped over the back of the couch and laid her head right in Enoch's lap and stretched her legs out.

They sat there in this position for a couple minutes, looking into each other's' eyes, not saying a word. Enoch kept a smile on his face while Karter just looked at him, all of a sudden the tears started to roll down both sides of her face. "Aw come on baby, don't do that to me." Karter having no control allowed the feeling to overcome her. It was like just hearing Enoch's voice broke a dam inside of her. She started to cry causing Enoch to feel guilty as well as make a real attempt to console her.

"I am here baby, don't worry." Enoch kept talking to her in this way as he leaned down to kiss her tear stained face.

Before long, Karter got it together Enough to speak. "Where were you?"

Enoch took a moment before replying. "Baby you know things got out of hand. I had to handle my business and almost got took out the game in the process." He lifted up his shirt showing her his bandaged chest and abdomen. This caused Karter to change moods to a look of concern. She gently rubbed the bandages while she turned into him to kiss his stomach.

"When did this happen?" she asked him.

"The same night I last talked to you. I got snaked out, but Ya Boy pulled through. I should thank you for the vest you bought me. Shit was too hot for me to even attempt contact. I am fucked up though cause I let the little change I did have slip through my fingers. Baby, please tell me you got some blow. I need a fix bad as a hoe need a trick!" Karter just laid there looking up at his face.

She felt there was something he wasn't saying, but she let it pass, knowing he would say nothing more. "I felt you." Enoch not understanding what she was saying just looked down on her with a dumbfounded look.

"I said I felt you. When you got hurt I felt it. I don't understand how or why, but I felt something in body. I called and called and got no answer. I called all hospitals as well as jails. It didn't take long to figure out that they didn't have you cause they kept flashing your picture on the T.V." She started crying again, so Enoch just sat and rubbed her face giving her time to finish. Right now Karter and his guilt had him held captive.

"I don't want to do this anymore." Karter managed to get out between sobs.

"Don't worry about that baby I got you." Enoch replied.

Karter just looked at Enoch and smiled. She made no mention to him about the baby and he didn't ask. Not having to trick and jack niggas anymore is more than she thought he would agree to. Hearing this changed her mood in an instant. She jumped up from the couch and ran and grabbed her purse from the off the floor. Enoch watched her as she now sat next to him rifling through her purse looking for the coke he had asked for. Enoch couldn't help but notice the stacks of money she had inside as well as her new car key.

"What's that?" he asked her.

"What?" Karter kept digging until she found the baggie filled with coke Enoch had previously asked her about.

Enoch reached into her purse and came out with her keys in his hand. He just dangled them in front of her face in a mock attempt to hypnotize her. Karter smiled at Enoch and waited for him to ask her what he really wanted to know.

"Who's keys are these Karter?" He finally came out and asked her. Karter took a few seconds before answering.

"Those are mine Boy." Enoch just sat there for a second admiring the Chevy key attempting to see if he could figure out the make and model.

"It's a Chevy Camaro in case you are wondering. I bought it about a week ago so I could travel around the city searching for yo ass."

"How much you pay for it?" Enoch asked her.

"Why you all in my business? All you need to know is that it belongs to me, and it is not stolen." Karter laughed at Enoch's expression after hearing her last remark.

"Aw you got jokes huh?" Enoch was really in his body. He wanted to know how much money Karter had spent. All his paper rode off into the night with Drako and he wanted to manage Karter's like it was his until he made it his.

"Well it's a good thing that you have the ride cause we gone have to get up outta this city for a minute. I have already hollered at Nice about us being able to flip our coins with him. He said he got some shit on deck right now, supposed to have some new connect. Sis and Jay gone have some paper for me in a few, days they say." He finished.

"They have been doing pretty good." Karter replied. "I was lucky enough to have a bird from the score on me, which I fronted to them. I called myself being cautious and leaving the bulk of what I got away with in a hotel room. I'm glad that I did cause them crazy muthafuckas had to have some sort of tracking device in that shit."

Karter cut in before he could keep going. "I am just happy that you weren't there. I don't know what I would do if something had of happened to you!"

Enoch, never allowing an opportunity to solidify his position pass him by, wrapped his arms around Karter buried his nose in the hair behind her ear.

"Nothing is ever going to happen to me baby." Enoch whispered in her ear while planting small kisses on her ear and neck.

They sat like this for a moment until Kelly walked in the door vibrant as ever. She was taken aback by the sight of Enoch sitting on the couch. She quickly recovered and greeted them both and went straight to the kitchen. In an instant she returned with a bottle of water in hand and sat on the couch right next to Karter.

"What yaw in here doing?" She asked before tipping the bottle of water back and taking a drink.

"Why you all in our business? Karter answered with a question of her own.

Kelly just looked at them both out the side of her eyes while taking another drink. When she didn't answer Karter asked another question of her own.

"Bitch where you been? I haven't seen or heard from you in a couple days." Kelly placed the bottle down on the table before answering Karter's question.

"I been with my new boo, since you must know. He super fine and super cool. He is from California and all about that paper."

"Bitch you better slow your fast ass down. These niggas out here ain't no good and only want one thing." Enoch told her.

"Is that so Enoch?" Kelly asked with a little too much attitude for Karter's liking. With that being said she got up from the couch, grabbed her bottle of water off the table, and made her way up the stairs.

"Damn she extra." Enoch said before wrapping his arms around Karter again.

"I know, but that's my cousin and I love her." Karter said while now leaning over the coffee table fixing lines of coke up for her and Enoch.

After both of them had gotten their noses dirty, they sat there for a moment in total silence. It was Enoch who spoke first.

"Baby we can go get a room and lay up for a few days. You know I can't wait to get another sample of that ass." Karter playfully popped Enoch upside his head after hearing that. Her ass had just healed from the ordeal at Jokers house.

"Boy you know you got me fucked up! My ass been tore up since I left the hospital." Enoch had a look of confusion on his face after hearing this.

"Right nigga! You did a little too much and tore the inside lining in my ass. Had me bleeding and everything. Only thing keeping me from smacking the shit out your stupid ass is the fact that I was able to use my bleeding as an excuse to have that fat muthafucka take me to the hospital. That's where I gave him the slip." Karter told him.

"Oh that's how you got up outta there?" Enoch asked feeling dumb for not asking earlier.

Karter just looked at him. The effects were wearing off from her just being happy to see him. She was now realizing herself that he never asked about how she managed to escape the house in one piece. She wondered would he even be here had he not lost everything in that room. She decided to just allow these feelings to pass and just enjoy his presence.

"So with that being said there will never again be any ass for you, but you can pay this pussy some much needed attention." Enoch just laughed at hearing her talk this way. From past experiences he knew that it was about to be some good couple days of sexcapade's. He dumped some more coke from the bag onto the table and snorted a line.

"Go get your shit together. We can take my car to get the room. I don't want to take a chance on getting your new whip hot, being that we will need it to get us to Dallas."

As soon as Karter got up Enoch smacked her right on her ass. Karter laughed and continued on her upstairs to gather her things. Her prayers had been answered. She had her Enoch back safe and was happy.

Chapter 33

*J*oker, Mondo, and Smoke were at the safe house enjoying the downstairs bar area. They had 5 of the most beautiful women Joker had ever seen butt naked, doing anything the men asked. Right now one of the women was upside down on the stripper, pole popping her pussy to the pulse of the music, that was playing out of the surround sound system. Two of them were standing on the bar dancing, while Joker was behind the bar pouring drinks.

He also had lines of cocaine on a mirror behind the bar for whoever wanted to partake. Mondo and Smoke were occupying the couches, both getting some head. They had a thousand dollar bet on who would come the fastest. Four minutes later as one of the women were draining all the cum Smoke shot out, it was clear who the winner was. Judging by the way Smoke was attempting to run backwards up the couch, it was no question as to if he had shot his load.

Mondo just laughed as he was pulling on the blunt of cocaine laced purple kush. Smoke had allowed an old dog to pull an old trick on him now he owed $1,000 of his weekly take. Things had been going well for them for the last couple of weeks. Working directly with Joker had its perks. They no longer dealt with local women.

The ones that were here now were flown in from California, compliments of the organization. No way was anything like what happened a couple of weeks ago to take place again or that was all their asses. Mondo was now fucking the woman doggy style, doing salsa moves at the same time. They were all having a good time enjoying each other's company.

Javier was out making runs for them, getting rid of the Meth that they retrieved from the hotel room. He had some contacts north of the river that had been buying 2 pounds a week like clockwork. Joker instructed them to make sure their business didn't interfere with his. Two of them had to stay with him at all times until things changed and they brought in fresh bodies. The brothers were in no rush for that because they didn't want to share their newfound wealth. They were all immersed in the activities paying no attention to what was going on outside...

****

Agent Jones was riding in the command vehicle with all 17 other officers going in the residence. They were going over their last minute briefing as they made their way to the target.

"We don't know who or how many may be inside, but we are sure Jose "Joker" Hernandez Chavez stays at this address. The utilities are in this name as well as two vehicles registered at the DMV. He has no priors so please restrain yourselves when we enter. Us obtaining this warrant was due to this being the original location, in which the money appeared to have been stored and tracked from. This doesn't make him guilty of anything so don't allow your emotions to cloud your judgement. Just make sure you are ready for anything and be the professionals I know you to be. We will work in three 6 man units, which we all understand will be made up of all of our different departments. I feel we should work better that way. My team is team #1; we will secure the lower level. Belton officers is team #2 and you will secure the perimeter. Team #3 will go in the back and secure the upper level. Try to stay off the radio unless necessary. I want don't this to turn into a shit show so be aware of what you are doing at all times. Any questions?"

Nobody said a word leading Agent Jones to believe that they were all ready. "Okay we will be arriving at the house in approximately 2 minutes, let's gear up...

****

The party downstairs was now looking like a porno. The women were now giving the men a show. They were all engaged in a full blown girl on girl scene. The men were all sitting on the couches, enjoying the view, and having a good time. BOOM!

Everybody jumped as the garage door was smashed in by the mobile battering ram. Each of the men went for their weapons, not computing what was happening. Before they could gather their bearings three federal officers had them at gunpoint, barking out orders. Joker and Mondo instantly dropped their guns on the floor. Smoke too under the influence to care raised his AK-47 only to be cut down by the officers like fresh fire wood.

"Get down! Everybody get down now!" one of the agents barked. The music was still loud causing them to have a problem communicating with each other. They used hand signals to operate. It took them no time to cuff, Joker, Mondo and all the women. An all clear came over the radio for the rest of the house. Agent Jones stepped into the room, looked down at Smoke lying there dead, and walked over to the bar.

He picked up the remote to the sound system and turned off the music. "Mr. Jose Hernandez you are under arrest for suspicion of conspiracy of murder of an officer. You will also be charged with any drugs and guns we find here. We have a warrant for your arrest for money laundering and tax evasion. Damn shame you allowed the tracker you put in that bag of money lead us right back to you. Everybody else here is also under arrest for now and your cooperation will be the deciding factor as to what happens to you in the future. Get them all up and out of here fellas. Get someone in here to take pictures of this body before you move it."

With that being said he walked off to help with the search of the rest of the house. Mondo just laid there next to Joker looking at another one of his brothers slain by the pigs. He couldn't be mad at Joker because he knew that it was his work that set the ball rolling for these unfortunate circumstances. He could only hope that Joker kept his mouth closed and played this by the code. Joker's mind was working in overdrive. He was sure they wouldn't find more than a brick of cocaine, and his gun. He could have his lawyer eat all the other bullshit the agent was talking about easily. He was tired anyway, a short break wouldn't hurt. He was just hoping Mondo or the girls didn't say anything. He would have them all lawyers by the morning..................

Chapter 34

*K*arter and Enoch were in their room at the American Inn, laid up, after a night of passionate lovemaking. The television was watching them when a news bulletin interrupted the program announcing a break in the case of the officers being slain at the Belton Inn motel. They reported that there were two people in custody who were believed to have had direct involvement. They didn't have any names but showed Joker, Mondo as well as the California girls being put in unmarked cars in handcuffs.

Enoch just looked over at Karter and smiled. Seeing this made him more comfortable with his present situation. The police, although most likely still looking for him, would not consider him public enemy #1. He jumped out of bed stark naked and went to the small table to snort lines of his concoction.

He had taken some of the coke Karter had and mixed it with some of the pills he had crushed up. Karter saw him do this the first night they arrived and told him he had lost his damn mind if he thoughts she was snorting that shit up her nose. She watched him snort it and seem to turn into a totally different person. He got kinda aggressive in nature when he once again breached the subject about her finances. When he saw that he was getting nowhere he allowed his agitation to show in the pounding he put on Karter's vagina during sex.

He was like the energizer bunny and he just kept going, and going, and going....... Karter saw his temperament and just went with the flow. While he thought he was pumping her into submission, each thrust was putting more distance between the two. The encounter was a direct contrast from what she experienced with Joker. If she didn't get anything of real value from the ordeal, she found out what passion was. She wasn't convinced if it was Enoch's behavior or the fact that she now knew better that had her uncertain and disengaged. But whichever one it was she knew to disguise her feelings until she figured it out.

Enoch was now sitting at the table staring at nothing, looking stuck on stupid. Karter made a silent vow to make sure she got her hands on those pills and get rid of them before they became the death of them both. After getting up and showered they were now both sitting at the small table in the room finalizing their plans.

"Look. Nice said he will sell us each bird for 30. I thought we had more to fall back on which is why I gave sis and Jay the one I had for 27. I wanted them to get some real paper as well as have room to undercut the market to build up their clientele. I hope to be able to get one or at least half for this jewelry. They already texted and said the money is ready so that's 27. How much do you have?" Enoch asked Karter.

Expelling a breath while appearing to be going over her finances in her mind, she replied, "I never counted the money you left me from out of last lash but I spent $18,000 of it on my car. I put $12,000 in my safe deposit box so whatever is left is in the shoebox over Keisha's. I haven't been spending anything but the tips I made dancing, as well as the little change I already had."

Enoch just bobbed his head up and down as he went over the figures. He picked up his phone and called Nice who answered on the third ring.

"What up?"

"The wifey told me to thank you personally for babysitting and that she hopes our three bad ass kids haven't been too much trouble."

"Nah. They have been a blessing to have around." Nice replied.

"Well we will be there tomorrow to pick them up." Enoch told him.

"Already! Say no more. I'll even have my baby cook you two up something special down south style."

"That's what's up. Tell her that we send our love." said Enoch.

"You already know." Nice replied.

With that being said the call was disconnected. Enoch had just placed an order for three bricks and Nice had confirmed that it was all good. Enoch and Karter got their things together and checked out of the room.

****

As they were leaving they were spotted by Javier coming out of another room making a drop off. The two would have never caught his eye if it wasn't for Jokers jewelry Enoch was sporting. Javier got on his phone as he watched the two unsuspectingly get into a mustang apparently getting ready to leave. His phone call went unanswered so he tried again.

This time the phone was answered by a voice he didn't recognize.

"Hello!" said the voice.

"Que Pasa Mi Amigo" replied Javier.

Whoever it was that had answered Jokers phone took too long to reply so he hurriedly disconnected. Javier had to take matters into his own hands and right now he was not planning on allowing this chance encounter to pass by without at least following these two and seeing where they led him. He hopped into his rental Chevy Impala and followed the Mustang as they rode off, out into the day's traffic.

****

Enoch and Karter were exiting the highway on Paseo and Independence Ave. When the passenger side of the vehicle was peppered by gun fire, causing the passenger door window to explode inward and the windshield to spider web. If Karter had not have been riding with her seat in pull recline she would have assuredly been struck by the bullets the Mustang was being riddled with. The same went for Enoch who instantly smashed his foot on the gas running through the red light.

He had his head ducked low in fear of being struck by a bullet causing him to veer into another lane, sideswiping the unsuspecting mother and her two children, riding in a Toyota Camry, headed to lunch. After noticing the impact, Enoch made a cautionary glance out his rearview mirror to see if whoever had been shooting at them was following. Karter was still laying there trying to stay as far as possible under the possible trajectory of a stray bullet.

When Enoch was satisfied that they were in the clear he stepped on the gas and headed towards Keisha's house. They made it around the corner from her apartment and left the car in the parking lot of an apartment complex, after removing their belongings and wiping it down. They made it to Keisha's safely, but not before Enoch had instructed Karter to play it cool and don't mention what had just happened.

He instructed her to go in, retrieve all the money from sis, as well as what she had put up and he would be in the Camaro waiting. Karter went in and did exactly as she was told, while Enoch sat outside in the car snorting some of his concoction. He was attempting to calm himself after such a close call. Twice in the last month the grim reaper had come knocking at the door only to get no answer.

This along with the effects of the drugs caused Enoch to feel invincible. He was also in a murderous rage because he wasn't used to being tried like that. Karter hopped into the driver's seat and handed Enoch a backpack with the money in it. One look at Enoch told her all she needed to know; now was not the time to say one word to him so she started the car up and hit the road to destination Dallas........

Chapter 35

Karter exited the hotel bathroom toweling her hair dry after her shower. Her and Enoch had made the long journey to Dallas non-stop so stopping to get refreshed as well as rested before going to meet Nice was something they both felt was a good idea. Upon seeing all the items scattered across the bed, while Enoch sat there reading some paper she had yet to make out, she stopped in her tracks.

"What the fuck Enoch? I told you that the Tony was GONE!! You rambling all through my purse like a dope fiend is crazy!!" Karter told him.

Enoch looked up at her from the paper he was reading, facial expression showing that he was angry about something. Karter didn't pay him any more attention as she grabbed her purse and started placing her belongings back inside.

"So you went and got an abortion and didn't tell me?" Enoch asked her. Karter stopped what she was doing and looked at Enoch like he was crazy.

"Bitch don't just stand there looking dumbfounded answer me!!" He yelled at her.

"Enoch wasn't it you who told me, "Fuck that baby we getting rid of that muthafucka anyway?" She said to him.

"Listen bitch, don't play with me. Why you didn't tell me that you got an abortion. Don't tell me your decision had a muthafucking thing to do with me cause the date on here clearly shows you got it done not knowing whether I was dead or alive!!"

Karter still trying to keep her composure took her time before replying. "Look Enoch. I don't know what this is all about because I only did exactly as you asked. You got me out here snorting this shit, robbinhg muthafukcas and constantly putting my life on the line for you!" Now the tears were starting to fall. "I had to kill my child due to the standard of living you subjected me to and the best thing you can do is question me about why I didn't tell you. You need to grow up and be a man cause right now you are on some little boy shit!" She said to him.

Enoch was no fuming hearing this. "Little boy huh? You wasn't saying that shit while you was all on this dick attempting to get me to plant another seed in you these last few days!"

Hearing this broke Karter's last strand of restraint. She walked up on Enoch, finger in his face, spitting out of words of venom.

"Nigga on yo dick? I never made one advance toward you. You so caught up on coke and pill your performance was nothing you need to be feeling good about!! As far as a seed what type of bitch would I be if I was looking to have a child with yo arrogant, disrespectful, unreliable, dope fiend ass?!? The only reason you in here going through my purse is cause you looking for a fix. Talking about your dick; I get better dick from the tricks you send me after!" Karter was pissed.

SMACK!!! Enoch had jumped up from his seat on the bed and popped Karter right in her eye causing her to drop like a sack of potatoes. "Bitch you must have lost your fucking mind coming at me like I am some sucka. You lucky I got love for you or I would really tear off into your ass!! Get yo ass up and get dressed so we can go handle our muthafuckin business bitch." He said to her.

Karter just laid there on the floor, in a ball, holding her eye. She knew what she said would push him over the edge but she couldn't contain herself. She was hurt. She was forced to get rid of her child because of a lifestyle Enoch had introduced her to and trapped her with. She felt less of a woman for not being strong enough to protect the fetus that had been growing inside of her womb.

Enoch bringing it up brought those feelings she tried to suppress, to the surface. Since he had no compassion and wanted her to feel pain she dealt him the same hand. If him striking her was the price she had to pay, then she was happy to have been able to pay the tab.

She got up from the floor and used to towel she had been wearing to staunch the blood. Using her free hand, she gathered all that she would need to get prepared to leave. She went to the bathroom and closed the door behind her. "Don't be in that muthafucka all damn day either!!" Enoch said to the door pacing the room like a caged tiger. He was in a foul mood and didn't want to admit to himself that he needed a fix to calm his nerves.

For the sake of having something to do he picked up his phone, called Nice and let him know that he could expect them to be there within the hour. After hearing Nice confirm that he was indeed at the spot waiting on their arrival, Enoch forced himself to calm down and just laid back on the bed, waiting on Karter to emerge from the bathroom.

Karter was now dressed standing in from of the mirror trying to mask the damage done to her eye. She had got it to stop bleeding but there was nothing she could do about the swelling or the fact that it had turned red. She was pissed at herself for losing control of her emotions as well as constantly putting herself in the position to be abused. She told herself that right now wasn't the time to do anything but focus on making it back to the city with the work they were headed to get from Nice.

She exited the bathroom, put her things in her bags, returned all her items that were all over the bed to her purse, grab her keys and without saying a word to Enoch, headed to her car. It didn't take Enoch long to get the point. He grabbed is rags, placed his guns on his hips and followed right behind Karter anxious to get to their next destination.

****

Nice was sitting in front of his 72-inch flat screen TV playing madden when he heard Karter's car pull into his driveway. He immediately put the game on pause and walked to his front door, puffing on a blunt of pure kush, to retrieve his guests. Enoch was the first of the two through the door and Nice gave him a pound with a half embrace with the blunt still in his mouth causing him to squint his eyes because of the smoke. Just as he took the blunt from his lips, Karter walked in eye looking like she had pink eye.

"Daaammn!! What happened to that eye?" Nice asked barely able to control his laughter. Karter just gave him an evil stare letting him know she didn't find anything funny. "My bad. My bad babe girl. What's good witcha?" Nice said while giving her a hug. He could sense something was off with her at the moment so he instructed her to go to the kitchen and get whatever food and refreshments she wanted.

Nice had a real soft spot for Karter. He secretly had yearned for her ever since they swung together as a couple. He never planned to allow these feelings to show cause Enoch was his mans and to him it would always be bros before hoes. As Karter made her way to the kitchen him and Enoch went to take care of business in the dining room. As soon as they entered Enoch's eyes lit up once he seen the 5 bricks sitting stacked on the table wrapped in brown tape.

"What's good my nigga?" Nice asked him.

"That there is $50,000. These are the pieces I was hoping to unload on you to cover the rest of the tab." Enoch was removing the jewelry from his neck, wrist and pockets as he said this. After checking it all over thoroughly Nice let out a breath through his nose before speaking.

"Bro you want to eat $40,000 for this? I will admit its very nice but damn!" Nice told him.

"Look my nigga that shit has to be worth at least 100,000, that bracelet alone gotta be worth 40 grand."

"Enoch I'm witcha on that but my plug deals in cash only. If I take that shit that means I bought it, either I wear it or sit on it till I can sell it. Neither one of those options are in my budget right now." Nice told Enoch.

Clearly agitated Enoch was on the brink of losing his cool. "So what can you do bro? Matter of fact what is this shit even hitting on?

"Bro you know I don't fuck around but I hear the shit that deal. You want to pop one open and see for yourself be my guest." Nice told him.

Enoch picked one of the bricks up off the stack and attempted to tear it open. Nice had re-fired up his blunt and was now laughing at Enoch due to the manner in which he was trying to get to the coke.

"Bro chill out, I gottcha." Nice said before leaving Enoch standing there while he went to the kitchen to grab him a knife. Upon entering the kitchen, he noticed Kater sitting at a stool at the breakfast bar. She just sat there nursing her glass of kool-aid as if she didn't see him standing there.

"Why the long face and down spirit Karter?" Nice asked her.

"I'm good Nice. Ain't nothing down in my spirits." Karter told him without ever bothering to look up at him and acknowledge his presence. Not liking her vibe and not just willing to let things go; Nice placed the knife he was holding on the countertop, reached over and put his hand under Karter's chin, lifting her face up, causing her to have to look him in the eye.

"Listen, whatever it is it can't be that bad. Be thankful that you are still here giving you to opportunity to make things better. Protect your peace Karter and whenever you feel like there is something you can't do alone call me and I got cha." Nice said to Karter.

With that being said, he took his thumb and lightly traced the outline of both of her lips trailing his way up around both eyes before drawing what seemed to be a heart between her eyebrows. POP POP POP!!!

Chapter 36

Q pod federal holding center CCA. "Jose Hernandez you have an attorney visit." Joker who was occupying one of the seats at the poker table quickly folded his hand and went to his cell to prepare himself for his visit. After being escorted through the halls to the visiting area he was directed to one of the private rooms where his attorney was already waiting, files open and spread out on the floor. He stood up to greet Joker as he came in the door.

"Mr. Hernandez. Pat."

"How are you?" Joker replied.

Pat Peterson is known to be one of the best fixers in the Kansas City metropolitan area. Murder, robbery, possession, conspiracy etc.; you name it he has defended it and well. After both taking their seats Joker broke the ice.

"Tell me you are here because you have scheduled me a bond hearing and that the prosecutor doesn't plan to object?"

Pat brought his head out of the file and just looked at Joker. When it was evident that Joker was serious he responded, "Mr. Hernandez I hope you are joking because if not you apparently don't know how much trouble you are in. I have copies of Miguel Sanchez's case file also. As you already know my colleague Dan Ross is handling his case and Mr. Sanchez has given written permission for all info pertaining to his case to be shared with you."

Joker cut him off, "Yeah, yeah, yeah. What do you mean I must be joking about the bond hearing?"

Pat not bothered at all by the interruption continued on. He opened the case files and started reading, "Okay so the money found at the scene of the Belton Inn shooting had a tracking device in it that federal agents reversed the technology to track it back to its original point of activation. This is what allowed them to fast track a warrant for your residence."

Joker just looked at Pat like he was crazy, waiting for him to tell him something he didn't know.

"After conducting a thorough search of your residence the agents recovered multiple weapons, thousands of dollars in case, almost a kilogram of cocaine, as well as DNA samples from an apparent large loss of blood that matches the DNA evidence found in the van used as an escape vehicle in the Belton Inn shooting." Pat stated.

Hearing this made Jokers eyes buck before he smacked his hand over his eyes shaking his head. His attorney continued with his report. "Miguel, who you refer to as Mondo, is willing to take the hit for the

Belton Inn shooting. He is saying that the blood came from two of his accomplices who died from their injuries sustained during the exchange of gunfire the with officers. He says him and Jesus Gabriel Lopez, who I am told goes by Ghost, were the only ones who lived through the ordeal. That was involved in the actual shooting. Now here is what I am really here to tell you. The feds want your cooperation! Even though Miguel is willing to take the wrap by himself, they still want your testimony to help tie up loose ends and also show that they really have this thing under control. I don't have to remind you that a lot of officers died for reason they believe you played a role in. Now I have your financial records which show you do legally have access to the types of funds recovered on the scene. What you don't have is financial records showing why you may have had so much in cash. The deal on the table is with your cooperation, you will only face charges for tax evasion and money laundering. You will forfeit any claim to the cash as well as the house." Pat finished.

"What the fuck you mean the house!?" Joker screamed while starting to sweat.

"The house." Pat repeated looking at Joker like he was crazy. "You won't be living in it anyway if you don't take this deal. I am not sure you realize how much trouble you could really be in. Conspiracy charges for one, if they decided to turn the money into drugs, considering they found a kilogram of cocaine in your residence. Using their drug scale, I am quite sure they could turn the cash into at least 30 more."

After saying this Pat just stared at Joker to make sure he got his point. "You should be looking at no more than 10 years. They refuse to offer a downward departure because they are not seeing to charge you with anything that could almost guarantee would give you a life sentence. Miguel already knows what's going on and wants you to take the deal. He finds it amusing that they are willing to offer such a good deal. He says even if he was to get out he would be deported and killed as soon as it was known that he was in Mexico. He says he will live like a king and run things from the inside."

Joker heard all that and although it made sense he just couldn't wrap his mind around letting the house go. His life was over also if he didn't find a way to retain possession of the house and get the drugs out of there. He would have to figure all that out later, right now he was forced to take a deal that was too good to be true. After finalizing everything with his attorney he returned to his unit no longer in the mood to play poker. His mind was now on doing 10 years and trying to find a way to get the house back...........

****

Javier sat in the back row of the courtroom with a clean cut, wearing a Brooks Brothers suit and tie. He knew he was taking a chance but he had to see his brother one last time before he was sent off to do a life sentence. After the judge gave his ruling and dropped the gavel the U.S. Marshalls escorted Miguel "Mondo" Sanchez to the courtroom side exit, him and Javier locked eyes transferring a message that went without saying. "Brother will be brothers no matter the circumstances."

Javier got up and left the courtroom after he say the door close behind his brother. He was now in the city alone. He had the cash him and his brothers had accumulated as well as about six of the bricks left from the Belton Inn fiasco. He was no surely the boss being that he was alone. He was already mentally putting a plan together on how he was going to take over the city, who he would use as the supplier, as well as where he would get help from. No way could he allow his brothers to have lost their lives in vain. The Hustle must go on. The saga must continue; is what he told himself as he hopped in the rental car and headed back to the city he would make his playground. "Killa City!"

Chapter 37

Present Day

I was roughly shaken awake. I came to starring my greatest fear directly in the face. Here was my male captor standing over me with no mask on confirming my worst fear. Last time I say this face it was showing me love, attempting to console me. The eyes that stared at me now told me that the love that once lived there was gone and had been replaced by an emotion far more sinister.

I could only lay there hoping that him now showing me his face didn't mean that it was time for me to die. He broke my train of thought with a one word questions, "Why?" I was too scared to answer cause I wasn't sure what he was asking me.

"Don't just lay there! Answer me!!" He said sternly to me.

I just stared back into his dark eyes searching for some clue for what I was expected to say. All of a sudden I heard the cries from the baby coming from upstairs. He broke eye contact, he looked towards the top of the stairs, then returned his gaze to me. I heard the sound of one of the upper stairs creaking revealing my female captor's position.

She was up there in the shadows eavesdropping on this conversation. I decided to break the silence between us with a questions of my own. "Nice, what is it you want me to say?" my heart was racing, I still couldn't believe that I was staring in the eyes of a dead man.

"Bitch don't call me that! That name has changed along with the way I once viewed you. You took advantage of the soft spot I had in my heart for you. You pretended to be in a bad situation just to get me to drop my guards. You and your man left me for dead in a pool of my own blood and for what? I would have given you what you took twice over with no second thought."

I just laid there looking at him with no words to say. My emotions were in an uproar because I felt what he was saying was true. Nice was the truth. Whenever we partied together, everything was on him. The swinging we did proved him to be a patient and passionate lover. He was the only one who ever questioned my blind loyalty to Enoch. I allowed Enoch to cross him without a second thought; I didn't even check up on him after I presumed him to be dead. I had to say something before I allowed my emotions to overwhelm me.

"Look I had no control, influence or knowledge of what happened that day. I was honestly distraught because he had just gotten done slapping me around. I was under the impression we were there to cop from you and get back on the road. Enoch shot you for reasons I still don't know or understand and literally drug me out of the house because I was in shock. Nice you have always been real to me and I always had spot in my heart for you." Nice just looked at me with a cold glare not letting on to what my words meant to him.

"As I told you once already, my name is no longer Nice, it's Menace. And bitch you think I don't know how many different niggas you and that bitch ass boyfriend of yours set up and robbed? I used to think that you were just a fly in his web but now I see that you may have been the one pulling all the strings the whole time. I see you got a new mark named Judah. I wonder what he would think if he knew your true nature? I will give you more than the chance you gave me. I will let you live happily ever after if you allow me to play Enoch's role in the next caper. I promise not to hurt or kill him." He said to me.

Hearing this come from Nice's mouth gave me hope and pain at the same time. How could I have been here this whole time and never thought of Judah. My recollection brought back the memory of him lying there in the middle of the floor bleeding. I wasn't even sure if he was still alive but I wasn't planning to divulge that information and kill my chance to get out of here alive.

"Ni, I mean Menace I had this planned out for myself. I have been planning my escape from this life for a while now. I have been allowing Judah to use the hair salon I manage as a way to launder his cash. He has a safe built in the floor under the desk in the office. There is never anything less than 200,000 in it. I can give you the combination to the safe as well as the keys and security codes." I let out to him.

"Bitch you been down here for the three weeks. By now your man has moved that money." Nice told me.

Tears were now streaming down my face as I processed his words while thinking of the last time I saw Judah. I would rather be drugged and incoherent than to have to face these memories with a clear mind. Understanding that I now had no other choice I had to reveal what I planned to keep secret.

"The night you took me from that van with Enoch, I was kidnapped by Enoch from my own birthday party and left Judah laying on the floor bleeding. I don't think he lived and if this is the case than I am sure the money is still there because nobody else has knowledge of its whereabouts." I explained to him.

"Oh so you and Enoch were once again about to ride off into the sunset with the loot and just like always before I happened to interrupt?" He asked in this condescending voice.

"No!! I swear to you it wasn't like that. I came to Atlanta in attempts to start over, only to be tracked down by him at the worst possible moment." I tried to convince him.

"You can stop the crying cause the tears won't get me to believe you, although I know that you are telling the truth. They had a memorial for your man a couple of weeks ago. He survived but was on life support for 3 days before dying due to the injuries he suffered. No funeral though. They shipped his body back to Jamaica for the burial. His friends and associates are very upset by this, being that they had money that hasn't been accounted for, invested into his drug empire. The word on the street is that you are responsible for all that happened that night. It didn't take long for this people to find out what tragic events like that were known to be left in your wake concerning the men you infiltrate." Nice said.

Nice/Menace just stood over me with a satisfied look on his face as he watched the news he had just delivered have its desired effect on me. I was crushed, torn up on the inside but I had to maintain my sanity in order to capitalize off of this situation if the opportunity presented itself.

"I already know what you are laying there thinking. You need to find a way to escape from here and make off with that case I am certain you weren't lying about; It's out of the kindness of the good piece of my heart that I have left that I offer you the opportunity to leave this situation behind you. Enoch and Judah are dead along with your past life! Me and you can make off with whatever cash and drugs you have knowledge of, giving us the chance to live the life we surely deserve. You can earn my trust by simply telling me where to retrieve what I am looking for."

I studied his face and saw the weakness he always had for me lying right there below the surface. I sensed no deception behind his motives. After analyzing my situation, I realized that I had no other choice; I had to lay a couple of my cards on the table.

"Nice I really need to you believe me when I say I am sorry about all that happened to you. My life had been a wreck after that until I ran away and came here. I was left with no choice to go along with things after he shot you or risk being killed myself. I remember that day and could tell by the look in your eyes that you wanted to save me then, as you do now. I am not sure I deserve to be saved but I am sure you deserve all I have to offer." I told him.

After getting it all out, I expelled a breath; released the weight of the world and also the knowledge of my past life off of my shoulders.

"The beauty shop that I manage is called Reflections. It's located down from the South Dekalb Mall on the Eastside. If you still have my belongings, then you should find the keys inside. I will give you everything you need to gain access to the building and the safe located exactly where I told you, under the desk in the back office. I am sure the assistant manager has been running the shop in my absence because this is how we operate. You go in after closing and should be able to find what you are looking for with no problem. I don't know where any drugs are because Judah kept that business to himself. I do have multiple safe deposit boxes that I can go to once I show you that you can trust me." I tried give him all the details.

After I finished speaking he turned on his heels and marched off up the stairs two at a time. There was a commotion when he made it to what I assumed to be the top. "BITCH what you doing up here sneaking around in the dark for?" He asked.

"Wasn't nobody sneaking!" Came the reply from the female voice.

"Bitch you up here quiet as a damn church mouse, eavesdropping and you talking about you aint sneaking! Get your silly ass in there with that baby and stay out of the way."

I heard heavy footsteps stopping across the floor over top of me. Hearing the voice of his female accomplice while I was coherent now had me convinced I knew her. I still couldn't put the pieces together mentally but that bitches voice was real and familiar. Nice came stomping down the stairs with a notepad and pen in his hand. He also had a belt, a syringe and a vial of the dope they kept pumping me up with.

He gave me the pen and pad and told me to write down any directions as well as information I felt he would need. When I was done and handed him the pad back, he apologized before drugging me telling me that hopefully this would be the last time. Being that down here is the basement I couldn't tell if it was night or day. I'm now assuming it's night cause he gave me the impression that he was headed out as soon as he finished with me.

I didn't fight as he administered the drug by now I had learned to fight the effects for what I thought to be 15-30 minutes, it all depended on if they fed me first. As I laid there with my eyes closed I heard him make his trek back up the stairs and across the floor above me. I was laying there drifting on this dirty mattress when I was brought to by my female captor.

My head was ringing and I was seeing stars as she stood over me with her gun in her hand. As I came to my senses I realized that she must have struck me across my face with her gun. By the look in her eyes I could tell that she was extremely angry and had plans to take her anger out on me. I just laid there while she assaulted me with all sorts of verbal threats and insults.

She had both of her feet planted on the side of me as she was bent over, in a rage, screaming in my face like Smokey on Friday. The gun she held mixed with her mental state had me in fear. After a few minutes I finally started processing what she was saying. "Bitch you think you the shit?? Bitch never will I allow your triflin ass to make off with another one of my niggas!! Bitch I will kill your stupid ass before I let that happen!"

WHAP!! Once again my head was ringing cause of another blow to my face from the gun she wielded. I never said one word. Judging by her mental state I knew it would be no use. Only consolation I had was that she was still wearing her facemask. I felt that this was a sign that said whatever she came down here to do she didn't plan to kill me.

As I gathered my bearings; I decided this may end up being the opportunity I was waiting for. Just as this thought crossed my mind, opportunity met up with proper preparation. She drew her hand back and brought it swinging down ready to strike and I lunged up with my hand burying the pen I secreted away earlier right in the side of her neck.

She dropped the gun and started stumbling backwards while wrapping both of her hands around her neck in an attempt to staunch the blood that instantly started pouring out. I tripped her with my feet before she could make it out of my reach. As soon as she fell I was on her searching for the keys to free me from my bonds.

After finding the keys, I was able to release myself from the chain but wasn't able to get the cuffs off. I picked the gun up where it had fallen on the side of the mattress and started to make my way towards the stairs. The cold concrete on my bare feet was almost enough to paralyze me, but I found the will power to continue on.

Just as I was about to place my foot on the bottom step I allowed my curiosity to override my sense of judgement. I trekked back and snatched the mask off of my captors' face. Laying there attempting to hold the blood in that was flowing out around the pen was a face I never in my life wanted to see suffer the type of agony she was now suffering from. I was shocked and hurt but mad as hell. I tuned on my heels and cautiously made my way up the stairs gun at the ready.

After reaching the top I moved room by room through the house searching for the exit. The rooms were dark but could tell that they were shabbily furnished. I bumped into a small table and knocked what appeared to be a small TV crashing to the ground. My ears were assaulted by the wailing cries coming from a baby laid somewhere near my position. I followed the sound, picked up the baby and with the baby in arms I finally made it to the front room.

After getting it unlocked and open I struck off down the street as fast as my legs would carry me. The street sign on the corner informed me that I was on Woodrow Ave. Too scared to stop moving I ran down the road for a couple of blocks hoping to run into someone who would help me. The adrenaline was wearing off and the drugs were once again taking effect.

I came to the corner of Metropolitan Ave and forgot to stop for the oncoming traffic that was now coming down the road. I was almost run over by the 95 Metropolitan Ave Marta on its way to the West End station. I just fell and laid there in a protective ball around the baby. I remember flashing lights, ghosts asking me my name and floating through the air before being placed on a spaceship. I saw a face, the last face I remember seeing laying on the floor squirming in agony. I had to ask her now that I had the change, "Why Kelly?"

To Be Continued.........................

We hope you enjoyed the read!! Let us know your thoughts about the book!!!!

Please leave a review at on our website:
www.eclecticpublishingllc.com

Also join our mailing list to be informed of all new releases and sales.

Join author T.Marie in her Facebook Group:
T. Maries Literary Mansion

www.ingramcontent.com/pod-product-compliance
Lightning Source LLC
Chambersburg PA
CBHW070055260626
47160CB00004B/1218